VENGEANCE IS MINE

I0638678

VENGEANCE IS MINE!

Ricardo S. Dubois

Edited by: Angela Hooper
Back photo courtesy Dwight Moore

VENGEANCE IS MINE

Copyright © Ricardo S. Dubois
All Rights Reserved
ISBN: 978-0-6151-6958-3

VENGEANCE IS MINE

INTRODUCTION

When John Braxton is released from prison after serving a ten-year sentence, terror strikes at the heart of the small community of Houma. Bodies of the men who were responsible for putting him behind bars begin to turn up dead. But not just dead! Brutally, sadistically tortured and mutilated.

His former nemeses worried they would be next! Each take precautions to prevent their inevitable demise. But one by one, from the shadows they are taken down. An unseen animal is on the prowl in the small community of Houma, taking its selected prey down one at a time, without mercy, without compassion. Will they be able to stop John in time before he kills everyone on his list? Or is he being falsely accused yet again! Will he be able to dole out the Vengeance that he has harbored for ten years, or will his plan be foiled?

VENGEANCE IS MINE

VENGEANCE IS MINE

Chapter One

John Braxton prisoner number 7526252, anxiously awaited his release. Ten years in a sewer that society set aside for misfits, thieves and murderers, had taken a gentle boy and turned him into a bitter man.

As a young man, John had hopes of going to college and making something of himself. But, as fate would have it, his future had taken an unexpected turn. Now he was getting the kind of education only a prison could offer.

An eight-by-ten cell had been his home for over a third of his life, the best years taken from him by a corrupt system that administered justice to fit the needs at the time.

John lay on his bed, reading the newly arrived letter, an invitation. It read:

THE TERREBONNE HIGH SCHOOL
GRADUATION CLASS OF 97
WILL BE HAVING THEIR TEN YEAR
REUNION

The invitation triggered memories of a time that seemed so long ago. Memories which John had all but blocked out of his mind. Memories of a time when he was not so hardened, and still innocent. John lay back on his bunk, a kaleidoscope of thoughts bombarding him. As his eyes closed, his mind

VENGEANCE IS MINE

drifted, drifted to a time ten years earlier, a time of innocence and hope.

Running down the empty hall, normally packed with students, John hurried to class. His normally reliable electric alarm clock had ticked its last at about two last night, resulting in his tardiness to class.

Each step he made echoed down the hall. He passed door after door until finally, he arrived at his English class door. Trying to stop a bit too abruptly, John slid past the door on the freshly waxed floor. Quickly back-tracking his steps, John grasped the door handle and entered.

Miss Peapot turned as the door opened, and looked in its direction, along with the rest of the class. Tardiness was one of Miss Peapot's pet peeves. John could remember vividly how she had totally humiliated a classmate on another occasion for being late.

He braced himself for the worst. Miss Peapot was a stereotypical old maid schoolteacher. Never married, Miss Peapot was absorbed in her work. An excellent teacher, although an excessive disciplinarian, Miss Peapot ran a tight ship. Her tightly pulled gray hair ended in a bun in the back, contrasting against her dark blue knee-length dress. Looking over her bifocal glasses, her stare was cold and hard. John knew what was coming next.

"Mr. Braxton," Miss Peapot started, "Why don't you tell me why thirty of your classmates are able to get here on time, but you are not able to?" She picked up her cane and waved it in the direction of the class, much like a fairy godmother would wave her wand.

VENGEANCE IS MINE

"I'm sorry," John started, "but my alarm --"

"CLOCK STOPPED WORKING!" Miss Peapot interrupted before John was able to finish.

"Yes," John said, looking out to the class for moral support. Blank stares greeted him.

"If I had a dime for every time I heard that one, I could retire!" Miss Peapot said, sarcastically.

John thought she was more than old enough to retire now, but remained silent.

"Go to the office and get a pass," Miss Peapot said, sighing and pointing to the door.

John knew from past experience it was better not to even try to argue.

Re-entering the hall, John took a leisurely stroll toward the office. Passing Lisa's room, John couldn't help sneaking a peek in. Standing at an angle where the class was visible through the narrow window in the door, but the teacher was not; John spotted Lisa on the second row. She looked totally bored as she stared at the teacher with her fist on her cheek, and elbow resting on the desktop.

Lisa looked beautiful as usual. Her shoulder-length hair was pulled back into a ponytail that hung just over the collar of her white blouse. Lisa had moved to Houma from New Orleans. She had only been here a short while when her father had suffered a heart attack and passed away. Since her dad's death, it was John who had been the rock she could lean on. This had brought them together and nurtured the love they now shared for each other.

Lisa did not spot John in the hall, but the girl next to her did. Recognizing John, she discretely leaned over and whispered to Lisa. Lisa looked at John and smiled that beautiful loving smile that could fill his

VENGEANCE IS MINE

heart like no other could.

John waved and was off to the office. The office was normally a busy place with students checking in or out for some reason, or for various other infractions which could land you a visit to the office. Thereby justifying their existence, John thought to himself.

Looking warily through the large glass window, which covered the entire length of the office, John walked through the office door. Slow day, John thought as he approached the counter.

"I need a tardy slip," John said, as the middle-aged brunette looked up from the papers she was sorting.

"Okay." She walked to the end of the counter to retrieve the sign-in log.

"Sign here," she said, pointing to a spot on the log, "and I'll fill in the rest of the information, address, phone number, reason for being late later," she concluded.

John quickly completed the sign-in, then laid the pen on the counter.

"Give this to your teacher," she said, handing him a small piece of paper she had been filling out while he signed in.

"Have a nice day," she added, as John turned away.

Returning to class, John gave the pass to Miss Peapot and took his seat. The hour dragged by at a snail's pace, until finally the bell rang, releasing him for a few minutes at least. John quickly found his way to Lisa's room, where she was waiting for him.

"Rough start this morning?" Lisa asked, as she handed John her books.

"Alarm clock," John responded.

"Yeah right!" Lisa laughed as they walked down the crowded hall.

VENGEANCE IS MINE

"Looking forward to tomorrow?" John asked, glancing at a sign taped to the wall advertising Senior Prom.

"I guess," Lisa said in a coy sort of way.

"You guess?" John asked in total exasperation.

Lisa smiled easing John's anxiety. Lisa liked putting John on the spot, and now and then playing with his head. But through it all, Lisa loved John with a burning all-consuming kind of love. This prom was to be their first, having only started seriously dating at the beginning of the school year.

Lisa was a very popular girl around school, guys asked her out frequently. John knew this, though Lisa had never mentioned it. It still annoyed John that these other boys, even though they knew the couple were going steady still tried to snake him.

John felt very fortunate to have a girl like Lisa. What was important to most girls her age when they looked at a guy were nice clothes, nice car, and lots of money to spend on them. This didn't attract Lisa to John, because John had none of these. John was baffled why she would spend her time on him, but he was wildly grateful. He knew a good thing when he saw it.

The bell rang, and the hall started to clear out. John saw Lisa to her door, then hurried three doors down to his biology class.

John hated this class most of all. It wasn't the subject John hated, nor was it the teacher. John dreaded this class because the three terrors of the school were all combined in one class: Fred, Paul, and Steve. Separated only by conflicting schedules, this trio had bullied the entire student body either into submission or total avoidance.

9

VENGEANCE IS MINE

Fred, seventeen, was the son of the local sheriff. Fred was used to having his way. Average height, with brown hair and brown eyes, Fred appeared to be a clean-cut all-American boy. There was only one problem - Fred was rotten to the core. Fred, along with his two sidekicks, Steve and Paul, had been able to manipulate everything, and everybody, to do their bidding. When his influence failed to bring the proper response, Fred would simply get his dad to make a phone call, which was precisely how he landed the position of quarterback on the school's football team.

Larry Rivera, a friend of John's, was by far a better athlete and overall team leader than Fred. However, after Fred's father had impressed upon the coach how alumni support was essential for a successful team - and that alumni influence could heavily impact the future aspiration of aspiring coaches - the coach had gotten the message. Larry was quickly sidelined, and Fred started as quarterback.

Fred's father's threats were to be taken to heart. As the head of the alumni association and as Sheriff, Fred's father wielded a tremendous amount of power and was not afraid to call in a favor. From judges to senators, Fred's father was on a first-name basis with them all.

The second problem was Paul, he was a lot heavier than Fred, not as tall but stocky. Muscularly built, Paul was the strong-arm of the trio. Just at a glance, Paul would also suggest a clean-cut, well-mannered young man.

Clean-cut? Yes. Well-mannered? Not hardly. Paul had beaten up and bullied any student that displeased him in the least. Easy fights he would walk away from unmarked. The harder ones were settled in

VENGEANCE IS MINE

the office with the second party always finding himself expelled as a result of the altercation. Paul's persistent and consistent obnoxiousness made him by far the most hated and feared of the three. Paul had no fear of the law. His father was the Mayor of the small town of Houma, and Fred's father was the Sheriff. It was well understood by everyone in the school that if you caused Paul trouble, his dad would cause you trouble, and he had the power and authority to do it.

Steve appeared like the odd man out. Always impeccably dressed, he sported around in a late-model Jag. Steve was not as arrogant or brash as the other two. Steve's parents were people of great wealth, and gave Steve everything he could ever want, except that they neglected him with their time. Steve had rebelled, which caused him to be expelled from an exclusive private school. After enrolling in public school, Steve had started hanging around with Fred and Paul. Since then, Steve did not have his own direction; all he did was follow.

To be in the same class with one of these three individuals was miserable, two was unbearable, and to have the misfortune to be in the same class as all three was unthinkable.

And that is precisely what John had. All three were in his class. Their favorite recipient of their abuse? You guessed it- John. John was slow to anger by nature, and had been able to repel their savage attacks by simply ignoring them. This had worked for some time, but lately Fred had begun to escalate his assaults on John from verbal to physical. Ever since Fred had been turned down repeatedly by Lisa for dates, he, with the help of his two sidekicks, had been determined to take it out on John.

VENGEANCE IS MINE

"Today's lab day," Ms. Gautreaux began as the class settled down into their seats.

"You will each be assigned stations, two to a station," Ms. Gautreaux concluded, taking out her station assignment sheet.

"John," Ms. Gautreaux called, "your assigned partner is not here. Since Paul does not have a partner either, you will share a station." Ms. Gautreaux looked back at her roster.

John looked over his shoulder to see Paul staring at him with an evil look, and slowly striking the palm of one hand with the closed fist of the other, simultaneously smiling a wide grin.

John felt trouble coming like a freight train, and he was powerless to derail it. John and Paul took their stations along with the rest of the class. For a while, everything was going smooth until Ms. Gautreaux left the room.

The action began all too soon. Fred hopped up from his chair and charged John in a tackle position, blind-siding him and sending him to the floor.

Caught totally off guard, and having the wind knocked out him, John was slow to regroup. Fred never said a word as he began to pepper John with a fury of fists.

John rolled Fred to his side and quickly got to his feet. Fred soon followed, charging straight into John. John mustered all his strength and swung with an uppercut landing squarely on Fred's nose. John felt the cartridge crack as he straightened Fred up, sending him sprawling backward.

At this point, Paul was ready to take over. He got out of his chair and started toward John.

"No!" Fred yelled, stopping Paul in his tracks. "He's

VENGEANCE IS MINE

mine!"

Fred got to his feet, bleeding profusely now from the nose. He started once again at John, much slower now, as if he had methodically thought out his every move. Fred had his right hand behind his back, concealing John knew not what, as his nemesis moved ever closer.

When Fred felt he was within striking distance, he pulled his hand from hiding, revealing a switchblade. John had crossed the line; he had humiliated Fred in front of others. For this he would pay.

Fred lashed out at John, causing him to jump backward, stopping with his back to a large table covered with various tests tubes and beakers.

John's mind raced furiously. He looked to his right for anything that would aid against the eminent second volley of attack, this time with a switchblade's sharp edge in front of him and he had nowhere to retreat.
John picked up a large graduated cylinder just as Fred moved in.

Making a large sweeping motion with the knife, Fred misjudged his distance by a fraction of an inch as his blade passed harmlessly by John. Fred followed through with the blade, and John brought the graduated cylinder down hard on Fred's head.

Fred fell to the floor, out cold.

VENGEANCE IS MINE

Chapter Two

Ms. Gautreaux entered the room just in time to hear the glass shatter as it splintered against Fred's head.

Paul ran at John and caught him with a series of blows to the midsection, bending him over and sending him to his knees. Steve ran to retrieve Fred's knife as Ms. Gautreaux entered the room.

Paul turned to the rest of the class, who had watched with horror Fred's assault on John. In a voice loud enough for them to hear, but soft enough to prevent Ms. Gautreaux from hearing, Paul said, "If y'all know what's good for you, you'll keep your mouths shut!" Paul concluded just as Ms. Gautreaux walked up.

"What's going on here?" she cried, as she walked up and saw Fred sprawled on the floor struggling to regain his senses.

"John jumped Fred!" Paul said frantically. "Fred accidentally bumped into John and he went berserk. He punched him in the face, and when he tried to get away, John hit him with the graduated cylinder. He's gone completely crazy!"

Ms. Gautreaux told one of the students to run get the principal. Moments later, two gentlemen in their mid-forties entered the room, followed by the school

VENGEANCE IS MINE

nurse.

The second gentlemen was the vice-principal, and along with the school nurse, he tended to Fred's wound.

After evaluating the extent and nature of the wound, the nurse decided to call an ambulance to take him to the hospital, "just in case," she said.

"Did anyone see what happened?" the vice-principal asked as he scanned the quiet class.

"I did!" Paul quickly responded.

"So did I!" Steve joined in.

"Anyone else?" the vice-principal asked, waiting a couple of moments for a response.

"All right then, you two come with me," the vice-principal instructed as he headed for the door.

John sat in the outer lobby of the principal's office, watching as Paul and Steve was escorted into the principal's office. Undoubtedly to give an unbiased, truthful account of the recent events, John thought sarcastically.

The vice-principal stood with his back to the counter, arms folded across his chest, staring at John with a look that warned John away from any further violence. A short while later, as John waited, Steve and Paul came out of the office and looked at John with a smirk that told John his fate.

The principal came out and motioned the vice-principal to bring John into his office. John entered and sat down in a chair directly in front of the principal's desk.

"John, I have to tell you," the principal started as he put his forearms on his desk, interlocking his fingers, "You're in a lot of trouble. I have two witnesses that said you picked a fight with Fred. When he tried to

VENGEANCE IS MINE

walk away, you clubbed him," the principal concluded.

"It's a lie!" John protested, but did not appear to dissuade the principal or the vice-principal.

"It's out of my hands," the principal said, in a cold emotionless tone. "The police are on the way. You will be brought downtown and held for bail." The principal concluded just as a door opened outside the office.

Two parish deputies had entered the lobby, slamming the door behind them. They wasted no time, heading straight for the principal's office.

The officers knocked, but before a response could be given, they were in the office.

"So you're the punk who likes to pick fights and hit people when their backs are turned," the younger of the two officers stated.

"He pulled a knife on me!" John protested, but he knew Fred's father, the sheriff, had sent these two.

The young officer turned to the principal. "Did anyone find a knife at the scene?" the officer asked, in a half hearted display of an investigation. Then reaching down, he pulled on John's arm for him to rise.

"No," the vice-principal responded.

"Were there any witnesses?" the deputy questioned the principal still further.

"Yes, two," the principal said as he handed the deputy two cards, apparently containing the names and numbers of Paul and Steve.

The deputy pulled John's arms hard behind his back as he handcuffed him roughly. The second deputy read him his rights and then escorted him out of the office. The officers brought John to the waiting patrol car and placed him in the back seat.

Sitting in the back of the patrol car, John sank low

VENGEANCE IS MINE

in his seat. Fred's father would see to it that his deputies allowed John no loophole, no way out. Things look bad, very bad.

VENGEANCE IS MINE

Chapter Three

There was quite a commotion outside, as the students congregated and murmured about the fight. Fights usually caused a stir, but rarely had a student gone to the hospital, with the other taken away by sheriff's deputies.

Class was totally disrupted as students offered possible causes for the unfolding series of events, as teachers fought their own compulsive urge to find out what was going on.

"What do you think is going on?" Lisa asked her girlfriend sitting next to her.

"Don't have any idea," her friend said, never taking her eyes off the door as she waited for any word about the strange happening. As Lisa's friend kept her vigilant lookout on the door, she recognized one of the passing participants. "It's John!" she exclaimed in a voice loud enough to make half the class turn and look at the door.

Lisa got up immediately and went to the door, opening it quickly. She made up the distance to John in no time but was intercepted by the principal.

"Go back to your room, young lady," the principal ordered

Seeing he had gotten no response, the principal

VENGEANCE IS MINE

ordered less politely, "GO NOW!"

Lisa turned to walk away as she could see John getting farther and farther down the hall, unaware of her presence.

Seeing that Lisa was going to comply with his last order, the principal turned and continued to walk toward the office.

Lisa had no intention of going back to class. At the first chance she was able to duck around a corner, she waited until the principal was well out of sight.

Back-tracking her steps, Lisa soon made her way to the principal's office. She remained out of sight but occasionally peeked a look and was able to see John through the class window of the office. John was seated; the vice-principal standing guard over him.

As Lisa watched, the door to the office opened, and out walked Steve and Paul! Lisa's thoughts were racing now. What did these two hoodlums dream up to get John in trouble she thought, as they opened the glass door into the hall. Lisa saw John being escorted into the principal's office, when Steve and Paul spotted her.

"Take a good look!" Paul told Lisa as he turned the corner. "It'll be the last time," Paul said, in his usual smart aleck undertone.

"What happened?" Lisa demanded. She stood stubbornly with her back to the wall with the two bullies standing before her, Paul with an outstretched hand leaning against the wall as he spoke. Steve just stared.

"Your little boyfriend almost killed Fred, that's what happened!" Paul said, as his eyes left Lisa's and began to scan her body.

"I don't believe you!" Lisa said. "You're lying!"

"Oh, it's true, Lisa," Paul continued. "The police are

VENGEANCE IS MINE

on their way over now."

Lisa was terrified for John. Tears began to roll down her cheeks, her down turned eyes staring at the floor in disbelief.

"Don't cry," Paul said as he lifted her chin with his free hand, looking her in the eyes again.

"A hot little number like you won't have any problem finding a replacement," said Paul, as Lisa slapped his hand from her chin and plowed her way through the bullies.

Lisa could hear Steve and Paul laughing as she headed down the hall. She had to help John, she thought. But how?

Passing the old wooden phone booth, Lisa stopped, opened the door, then sat down to regain her composure. She was crying a lot harder now.

Lisa had left the class in such a hurry that she had forgotten her purse, realizing it only after she looked at the phone. She removed her right shoe and found the quarter that she had carefully taped to one side. Her mother had impressed upon her: Always have quarters in your shoe in case you need to call home. Lisa could almost visualize her mother saying this once again for the millionth time and she smiled through her tears.

Lisa deposited the quarter and dialed the number, annoyed at how long the rotary dial took to return to its original position, ready for the next number.

It was ringing now, Lisa waited for an answer, four times, no answer.

"Hello," a pleasant-sounding voice responded from the other end of the receiver.

"Mrs. Braxton!" Lisa said, her voice filled with tears.

"Lisa, what's wrong?" John's mother asked,

recognizing her voice.

"It's John," Lisa started. "He's in trouble, the police are coming, Fred's in the hospital," said Lisa, unsuccessfully attempting to explain the situation to Mrs. Braxton.

"Where's John now?" John's mother asked in a less pleasant, sterner voice.

"He's in the principal's office right now, but the police are coming for him," Lisa said as she finally regained her composure and began wiping the tears from her eyes.

"Lisa, I'll be there in twenty minutes," Mrs. Braxton said. Not waiting for a response, she hung up the phone.

Looking at her watch, Lisa decided to wait in the booth rather then standing in the hall risking being seen and sent back to class.

Time dragged by slowly as Lisa waited and wondered to what extent Fred was hurt. Not out of concern for Fred, of course; Lisa felt Fred had finally gotten what he deserved. Surely, the punishment to John would not be that great if Fred was not hurt too bad.

For twenty minutes, Lisa guessed and second-guessed on Fred's condition; not knowing was driving her crazy. She would have called the hospital, but she had used her last quarter. All she could do was wait and hope.

The twenty minutes had finally passed by her watch.
Lisa left her hiding place and started back to the principal's office to meet Mrs. Braxton.

Lisa reached her original observation point and was surprised to see Mrs. Braxton already in the office

VENGEANCE IS MINE

shaking her finger at the principal and verbally assaulting him.

John was gone! He had evidently been taken away while she hid in the phone booth.

Lisa walked right up to the office door and opened it.

Upon seeing Lisa enter, Mrs. Braxton stopped her conversation with the principal and turned to Lisa.

Lisa went up to her and hugged her, at the same time asking, "Where's John?"

"He's been taken downtown to sheriff's headquarters," Mrs. Braxton said. "I'm going there now."

"I want to go with you!" said Lisa in a determined voice that would not take no for an answer.

"Very well," said Mrs. Braxton in an equally determined voice.

Driving to the sheriff's office, Lisa could not help notice the excessive speed at which Mrs. Braxton was driving. Normally very conservative and overly cautious, Mrs. Braxton threw caution to the wind now as she hurried to her son's aid.

"What did they arrest John for?" Lisa asked, hoping to gain a better insight into what Steve and Paul had volunteered.

"Lies!" Mrs. Braxton exclaimed. "It's just a pack of lies! They say John picked a fight with Fred, and when Fred wouldn't fight, John hit him over the head with a bottle." She was visibly shaken and upset as she said this.

"That's crazy," Lisa said, reinforcing Mrs. Braxton's determination.

"I called Mr. Braxton when I was at school. He should be there when we get to the office."

VENGEANCE IS MINE

Arriving at a large brick building, which doubled as a courthouse and jail, Mrs. Braxton circled the block looking for a parking place. The courthouse comprised an entire block, and was by far the largest building in the small rural town of Houma.

After finally finding a parking spot, Mrs. Braxton parked the car. Then with Lisa close at hand; they hurried to the jail processing room.

Each step they made echoed in the long corridor leading to the processing room. The polished floors reflected their images as step after step brought them a little closer to their intended destination.

The old wooden door with its etched glass read, "SHERIFF'S OFFICE," in large bold print. Just under it in smaller letters was "Processing." The ladies entered the room and walked up to the large counter, which acted as a partition to separate the office from the lobby.

Mrs. Braxton went right up to the mature woman filing forms. "I've come here for my son," Mrs. Braxton demanded as the little old lady looked over her bifocals, not shaken or stirred into action by Mrs. Braxton's demands.

"Name?" the bifocal lady asked in a tone that indicated her annoyance at being inconvenienced.

"John Braxton," Lisa burst out. Realizing the way she had stepped over Mrs. Braxton, she withdrew and allowed John's mother to gather the information about her son.

Just then, Mr. Braxton appeared, coming out of a door located behind the counter on the opposite wall. He was escorted by a police officer as he headed to meet his wife and Lisa.

"Did you see John?" Mrs. Braxton asked of her husband. "Is he all right?" she asked quickly.

VENGEANCE IS MINE

"Yes," Mr. Braxton responded gravely, "they are trying to set bail now," Mr. Braxton explained.

"What did John say happened?" asked Mrs. Braxton, continuing to question her husband.

"Fred tackled John in class and started beating him. John fought back, then Fred pulled a knife." Mr. Braxton raked a hand through his thinning hair. "John hit him on the head with a glass cylinder."

"Were there any witnesses?" Lisa asked, looking around Mrs. Braxton to John's dad.

"Two, Paul and Steve." said Mr. Braxton, knowing the boys' reputation and loyalty to each other. Mrs. Braxton knew now the quagmire her son was in.

"Out of the whole class?" Mrs. Braxton questioned, "There were only two witnesses?'

"No!" said Lisa. She realized the predicament John was in. "There were more, but they won't say a word," Lisa stated, anger flushing her cheeks.

"Why?" asked Mrs. Braxton.

"Three reasons," Lisa offered. "Fred, Paul, and Steve."

She looked from Mr. Braxton to Mrs. Braxton. "Those three bullies have a stranglehold on the school, just like their fathers have a stranglehold on this town." She could barely keep her anger in check long enough to explain.

"The kids are scared to death," Lisa continued. "If they go up against the three, there's no telling what those bullies would do. Besides," said Lisa, "what good would it really be for them to risk themselves to the harassment which would surely follow? When the fathers of the three bullies are the Mayor, Sheriff, and have the financial resources of Steve's father, the

VENGEANCE IS MINE

verdict is already in."

Lisa wept now. As Mrs. Braxton put her arm around her, Lisa put her head on Mrs. Braxton's shoulder and continued to weep.

Mr. Braxton was more shaken by the truth of Lisa's words then he would let on. Tiny beads of sweat began forming on his forehead as he excused himself for a moment and left the waiting room to the hall in search of a water fountain.

The pain was increasing as Mr. Braxton located a water fountain. Reaching into his pocket, he removed a small bottle of glycerin tablets, taking one from the bottle and then returning the bottle to his pocket. The stress of recent events was taxing him far beyond the stress factor his doctor had cautioned him about.

Forty-eight years old, he had already had two heart attacks. Though minor, they had been a warning to him to slow down. Mr. Braxton tried to follow the advice of his doctor, especially when it came to diet.

Work, however, was a different story. Owning a small hardware store most of his adult life, Mr. Braxton had seen business go from good to just barely making a living. Longer and longer hours were needed just to keep up. Mr. Braxton knew he was pushing himself too hard, but he had no choice.

The pain in his chest began to subside; at times, the pain was severe, as though someone was shoving an ice pick into his chest. At other times, there was only a slight burning sensation. Mr. Braxton knew he had to go back to the doctor and take care of it, but he had put it off. Maybe, he thought, after this thing with John is over, maybe then.

Mr. Braxton returned to the office to find Lisa and Mrs. Braxton standing at the counter. Mrs. Braxton was

VENGEANCE IS MINE

looking over some papers as Mr. Braxton walked up beside her.

"Bail was set at one-hundred-thousand," Mrs. Braxton said as Mr. Braxton walked up.

"What?" Mr. Braxton exclaimed, shocked at the size of the bail. "Murderers get out for less," said Mr. Braxton, still reeling from the size of the bail. "What's the form for?" Mr. Braxton asked as he to began to look over the papers.

Mrs. Braxton turned to Lisa, "Lisa would you excuse us a moment," she said, taking Mr. Braxton across the room to talk.

"We don't have twenty thousand dollars!" Mr. Braxton said as a look of despair came over him. "A lifetime of work and I can't raise enough money to get my son out of jail!"

The frustration and stress was obviously getting to him as his mind raced for option. "We'll put the house up," said Mrs. Braxton. In place of the twenty thousand, or the ten percent a blood-sucking bail bondsman would charge, this option seemed the most practical. Mr. Braxton read the form well before singing it. The only risk to the house was in the event John did not show up for court. To Mr. Braxton, that was no risk at all. He knew his son wouldn't let him down.

After signing the necessary papers, Mr. and Mrs. Braxton, along with Lisa, waited for another hour, until John finally appeared in the lobby.

The reunion was brief. All those present were very anxious to leave the station. Outside, John's father separated from the rest, saying he would see them tonight. He had to reopen the store.

Mrs. Braxton, John and Lisa piled into the car and started home. Upon reaching their house, John and

VENGEANCE IS MINE

Lisa went to the living room. Returning to the living room with a large tray of sandwiches and tea, Mrs. Braxton sat across from Lisa and John, who were sitting together on the couch.

"I'm sorry I put you and Dad through this," John started as he tried to explain.

"If it had been anyone besides those three hoodlums," Mrs. Braxton said, at this point visibly angry, "this would never have happened."

John and Lisa each picked a ham sandwich and began to eat while Mrs. Braxton told them what she had been talking to the principal about when Lisa had seen her in his office.

"Kids," Mrs. Braxton said, as she crossed her legs and leaned back in her chair, "I've got more bad news, I'm afraid. You've been expelled, John," Mrs. Braxton said, pausing before dropping the other shoe.

"This means you will not be allowed to attend the Senior Prom," Mrs. Braxton concluded, knowing full well the impact this would have on John and Lisa.

"With all that's happened, I forgot all about the prom," John said, as he looked at Lisa, knowing her disappointment and seeing the way she tried to conceal it.

"So what?" Lisa said. "We can go out to dinner and a movie instead."

"Great idea!" said John, as he tried to conceal his disappointment from his mother.

After spending the rest of the afternoon at John's house, it was time for Lisa to leave.

Lisa lived only about two blocks away, so they decided that since it was such a pleasant day, they would walk.

"Mom," John called to his mother in the kitchen,

VENGEANCE IS MINE

"I'm going to walk Lisa home."

"Okay, dear," Mrs. Braxton called out, never leaving the kitchen.

The day was beautiful enough for John to forget his troubles, at least for a little while. Lisa and John strolled down the street holding hands as John would occasionally point out a squirrel or bird to Lisa, as he often did.

Reaching Lisa's house, John walked her to the door.

"Thank you for standing by me," said John, still holding her hand, but now looking into her deep blue eyes.

"I'd stand by you no matter what," Lisa said, leaning over to give John a kiss.

"You're real disappointed about the prom, aren't you?" John asked the probing question, trying to find out if Lisa had any hidden resentment.

"Sure I am," said Lisa. "but as long as I'm with you on prom night, it doesn't really matter.

"See you tomorrow," she said as she opened the door. "Pick me up at 7:00." She smiled and went inside.

Lisa had a way of making John feel like a million bucks. Her words could elevate him to levels he had never thought possible. Now John saw another side of Lisa because of this mishap with Fred. John knew how much Lisa loved him; a love not expressed in words but in deeds. She stood by him and would remain by him. John knew at that point that he could never love anyone but Lisa.

VENGEANCE IS MINE

VENGEANCE IS MINE

Chapter
Four

Fred looked up from his hospital bed at his two comrades, "I'm gong to kill that son of a bitch!" Fred yelled angrily, his hands clenching spasmodically into fists. The pain pills he had taken a short time earlier had not yet begun to work. His head continued to throb with pain, making him angrier still.

"I've got something for you," Steve said, reaching into the back pocket of his jeans. Looking toward the door to make sure no one was coming, Steve tossed the switchblade to Fred. Fred caught the knife and held it in front of him. Pressing a button, the blade flipped out and locked in place with a loud click.

"Great!" Fred said, in a much calmer tone than before. "Did anyone see you?"

"The whole class, but they won't say anything," Paul said.

"How about the principal, did he buy your story?" Fred asked, trying to cover all his bases.

"Sure did," Steve said. "Oh yeah, one more thing, John is expelled from school. He can't attend Prom or Graduation. They're going to mail him his diploma."

"Damn!" Fred protested, "I was hoping I'd see him tomorrow. We have a little unfinished business." Fred momentarily retreated into deep

VENGEANCE IS MINE

thought.

"Don't worry," Paul said, slapping his fist into the palm of his hand, "we'll get him."

"You said tomorrow?" Steve asked. "Is the doctor going to let you go?"

"Sure," Fred said, "it's not that bad, a slight concussion. They're keeping me overnight for observation, that's all."

"That's great!" Paul said as he stepped closer to the bed with an outstretched hand. "We're going to split now, but we'll be back tomorrow when they release you."

"Okay, dude," Fred said, reaching up to shake Steve's hand.

After Paul and Steve left, Fred thought about what had transpired that day. Fred knew if nothing else, John would pay for the humiliation he had caused him, and he would pay in a big way.

Fred also thought about Lisa and how she had turned down every attempt he had made toward her. Never before had any girl ever done this to Fred, and he became obsessed with having her. Not that he would want to keep her for a long-term arrangement. Fred just wanted Lisa long enough to conquer her, like he had so many other girls. He wanted Lisa's notch in his belt, and was being driven by that want.

Fred was determined one way or another that he would have Lisa, whatever it took. Fred settled back onto his pillow, trying to clear his mind of the thoughts that prevented his sleep. The thoughts, mostly of John, were scenarios of possible encounters. Encounters which had not yet happened. Encounters in which John would be the big loser. Fred's last conscious thought was of John, lying on the ground bleeding

VENGEANCE IS MINE

profusely as he begged him for mercy.

Friday arrived like an old friend. You knew it was coming and couldn't wait for it to get here.

John pressed the doorbell to Lisa's house and waited. The door soon opened, not by Lisa, however, but by her mother. "My!!" Mrs. Duet said. "Don't we look nice!" Mrs. Duet was referring to John's dark blue suit bought specially for the prom. John was decked out, from his highly polished shoes to his neatly combed hair. John looked very different, out of his everyday blue jeans and tee shirt.

"Come on in," Mrs. Duet said, holding the screen door open for him to pass through. "Have a seat," she said, pointing to the sofa in the living room.

Mrs. Duet was a pleasant-looking lady in her late thirties. The years had been kind to her; she was able to retain her beauty and youthful appearance. Looking at Mrs. Duet, one could not help but see the resemblance Lisa had to her mother. Both had blonde hair and blue eyes, but the real similarities came from the facial features. Widowed now for almost a year, Mrs. Duet's whole life now revolved around Lisa; her only child in the nineteen-year marriage, Lisa was Mrs. Duet's pride.

"I heard about your trouble yesterday," said Mrs. Duet, "those boys need to be locked up! They have been terrorizing the kids at that school long enough!" Mrs. Duet was obviously very passionate about the subject.

"Well, hello," a voice from behind John called.

John turned and saw Lisa standing by the door. She was wearing a short-sleeve white dress, which came down just to the knee. The skirt narrowed from

33

VENGEANCE IS MINE

the bell-shaped bottom to fit snugly at the waist, and her ample breasts were accentuated even farther by the low cut of the dress.

"You look great!" John said, as he walked over to her, taking her by the hand.

"You kids have a good time," said Mrs. Duet, as John opened the front door to leave.

"Don't wait up, Mom," Lisa said, she and her mother smiled at each other just before John closed the door.

Lisa and her mother had an understanding. Her mother would not be unreasonably strict with a curfew time as long as Lisa remained responsible for her actions Mrs. Duet was not so old as to forget what it was like to be with someone you cared for as much as John and Lisa did. Mrs. Duet remembered when she was dating Lisa's dad, how the night would end when it seemed it had only just began. Those memories of her late husband more than anything else caused her to be lenient with Lisa.

Lisa and John looked over the menu, as the waiter patiently waited to take their order.

"I'll have the filet minion," John said as he closed the menu and handed it to the waiter.

"And for the lady?" the waiter asked, after he had finished noting John's order.

"I'll have the same," Lisa said, as she too handed the waiter the menu.

"What did you think of the movie?" Lisa asked, as she caught John staring at her.

"A little too mushy for my taste," John replied, noticing Lisa's surprised expression.

"You didn't think it was romantic?" asked Lisa, as she further tried to enforce her belief that the movie was

VENGEANCE IS MINE

great. Waiting but not getting a response from John, Lisa said, "Well?" Seeing that she was not going to persuade John. "I thought the acting was superb," she said, goading John a little.

Another thirty minutes passed, with their meals arriving shortly thereafter.

After enjoying their meal, Lisa and John walked back to John's car. Opening the driver's door, Lisa slid over to the middle of the seat.

John slid in beside her, putting his arm around her and closing the door behind him. "Do you know how much I love you?" John asked, leaning over to kiss her, not waiting for a response.

Lisa and John kissed passionately as their young bodies began to warm with the fire of their desire.

Just then, headlights illuminated the entire inside of the vehicle, as a car turned into the parking lot. Lisa and John broke their embrace, startled by the sudden flood of light.

"Do you want to go somewhere where we can be alone?" John asked, as his stomach knotted up with tension, waiting for her response.

Lisa paused for a moment before answering. She surely didn't want John to think she was the kind of girl used to being taken off, parking. But on the other hand, she would enjoy spending an uninterrupted kissing session with John.

"I think so," Lisa said shyly. "Maybe for a little while."

John started the car and headed out of town.

VENGEANCE IS MINE

VENGEANCE IS MINE

Chapter Five

Fred, Paul and Steve had spent most of the night with their dates, and drinking whiskey they had smuggled in their coats. Fred's date, a pretty brunette who Fred had had before, was spending most of her time warding off Fred's groping. With the night winding down, the three decided to exchange their empty bottles with a replacement from the local liquor store, then cruise the town, and maybe later get lucky with their dates. Going in two cars, Fred and Paul rode with their dates and Steve and his date followed in his convertible two-seater car.

Arriving at the liquor store, Fred went in to purchase. Out of the three, Fred had always had the least trouble getting whiskey. Just as Fred was coming out of the liquor store, he saw John and Lisa heading out of town. A burning, all-consuming anger rushed through him and he ran over to Steve's car.

"Paul and I will take your car," Fred said, turning to Steve, who along with their dates had gotten out of the car.

"After you drop them off, come back here, and I'll call you on your car phone and let you know where we went," Fred concluded, as his bewildered friends complied with his instructions.

VENGEANCE IS MINE

It had always been a good rule of thumb to never cross Fred, or to question too much at the time action was needed.

Paul and Steve didn't know exactly what was going on, but they knew it was extremely important to Fred. Steve, taking his date by the arm, turned to Fred's car and addressed the other girls that had gotten out of the car, hearing Fred's excitement.

"The party's over, girls," he said, as he opened his door for his date.

Fred drove out of the parking lot, kicking up gravel as he went.

"What's up?" Paul asked as Fred turned the car out of the parking lot and headed out of town.

"I just saw John and Lisa," Fred explained, as the speedometer needle quickly climbed.

"This is the night!" Fred yelled. "That son of a bitch will wish he was never born!" Fred screamed over the roar of the engine.

The highway heading out of town was a straight one. Lined on both sides by sugar-cane fields, the road offered just a few dirt road turnoffs, which led into the cane fields and then dead-ended.

Fred knew about how much of a lead John had gotten on him as he floored the sports car, trying to close the gap. Seventy, eighty, ninety miles an hour, Fred pushed the convertible, as the cool night air rushed through their hair.

There was virtually no traffic at eleven-thirty at night, and the clear sky offered an unobstructed view far, far down the highway. Fred saw no lights. Surely, he thought, he must have been able to catch up to them by now. Fred pulled the car to the side of the road, much to Paul's relief; he had been holding his

VENGEANCE IS MINE

seat with a death grip, bracing himself for the crash he knew would come.

"Any ideas?" Fred asked Paul, his mind racing, searching for a possible solution.

"Unless ---," Fred said, more like talking to himself rather than to Paul.

Fred said no more as he turned the car around and headed back to town, much slower this time.

"Look down the dirt roads," Fred ordered as he slowly passed them on their return trip to town.

Turning off the headlights to avoid detection, Fred eased the automobile across the lane that entered the cane field. Driving past, they scanned the roads for John's car.

"They more than likely ducked down one of the roads," Fred suggested, as he strained his eyes into the darkness, hoping to get a glimpse of an outline of a car, a reflection of a taillight, or anything that would disclose John's hiding place. The moonless night offered little assistance in their quest as they moved slowly down the highway.

"Wait!" Paul exclaimed, "I think I see something!"
Paul started to open the door to get a closer look when Fred grabbed his arm.

"Let's get off the highway first," Fred explained as he pulled up to another dirt road about fifty yards away on the opposite side of the road.

Fred parked Steve's car, then along with Paul, ran across the highway to the edge of the dirt road they had passed just moments earlier. Reaching the dirt road, Fred and Paul peered around the edge of the cane.

"There it is," Fred whispered as he nodded to Paul.
"Let's go back and call Steve," Fred said, as they turned back toward Steve's car.

VENGEANCE IS MINE

"Let's get him now!" Paul pressed, anxious to finish what he hadn't been able to in biology class.

"Patience," Fred said, in a calm, methodical manner, back at Paul who was walking a step behind him, still sulking because he did not get his way.

Paul sat anxiously in Steve's car as Fred punched in a series of four numbers on the cellular phone.

"Information - what city?" the operator's voice came
through the phone.

"Houma," Fred replied.

"Yes," the operator pressed him for further information.

"Could I have the listing for T-Bob's Pack-A-Sack," Fred asked, as he peered up into the dark sky, only then realizing how many more stars could be seen without the lights of the city.

"2-9-2-3-8-6-1," a computerized voice said flatly. Fred pressed the button to disconnect, then dialed the number for the Pack-A-Sack.

"T-Bob's Pack-a-Sack," a rough voice echoed through the receiver.

"Yes, is there a fellow by the name of Steve there?" Fred asked in a pleasant, disarming tone.

"Hey! Your name Steve?" Fred heard the attendant ask, then heard the phone being laid down on the counter.

"Hello," Steve's familiar voice answered.

"Steve," Fred started, cocky and confident. "we've got the son of a bitch!" he said, looking over to Paul, who was still visibly anxious to get to John.

"Where are you?" Steve questioned, not knowing whom he was talking about.

"Come down Highway 90 heading out of town.

VENGEANCE IS MINE

We're about eight miles out. And don't drive too fast. We're off the road," Fred explained.

"Off the road!" Steve exploded, suddenly worried about the condition of his car.

"Don't worry about your car," Fred scolded. "Just get here!" Then he hung up the phone.

Fred and Paul got out of the car and walked to the edge of the highway. They did not have to wait long, as Steve drove up, turning onto the narrow dirt road and parking behind his own car.

Getting out of the car, Steve rushed back to Fred and Paul, who were still waiting by the highway.

"How do you want to play this?" Paul asked, as Steve walked up.

"We'll go in through the cane field," Fred explained, using his hands to gesture their intended movements, "Staying parallel with the dirt road until we are even with the car. Then," Fred said, as he bent over and picked up a rock the size of a softball, "we'll shatter the window and drag the prick out of the car."

The trio crossed disappeared into the cane field.

John kissed Lisa with a burning passion, as she reciprocated in kind. The innocence of their young love warmed their bodies as they embraced each other. John longed for the day he and Lisa would share their love without restrictions or bounds, but for now John had disciplined himself to be satisfied with kissing, not wanting to rush or pressure Lisa.

The radio was the only light in the car, with its soft green glow providing just a light illumination. The night was cool, but their bodies had warmed the inside enough for John to partially roll down the window of his locked door.

VENGEANCE IS MINE

While Lisa and John kissed, the tape player rolled out a selection of soft, romantic music.

"What was that?" Lisa straightened up. "I thought I heard something," she persisted further.

"You just heard the radio," John said, trying to reassure her.

Lisa was scared, out in the middle of nowhere. A sinking feeling came over her, a premonition of something bad happening after all their ill luck. All Lisa knew was that it was time to go, *Now!*

"I want to leave now!" said Lisa, in a stern but shaken voice.

John knew she would not reconsider. Something had scared her, and scared her bad.

"Okay," John said, straightening up on the seat. Reaching for the ignition, John said, "We're out of h----" Before John could finish his sentence, a crash of shattered glass broke the silence. Something large struck John on the shoulder, sending glass throughout the interior of the car.

Chapter Six

It had seemed not more than a second after the glass on the driver's side had shattered. Then a set of powerful arms had him firmly in their grip, dragging him out of the open window. Lisa screamed in horror.

Having John most of the way out of the car, Paul slammed John's dazed body to the ground. Reaching down, Paul pulled him to his feet, then grabbed him in a full Nelson.

By this time, Lisa was out of the car and running to John, but Steve grabbed her.

Paul threw John to the ground as Fred turned to Lisa. Grabbing her by her long blonde hair, he jerked her head back.

Steve, by this time, had let go of Lisa and walked over John's motionless body.

"You don't look so high and mighty now, bitch!" Fred said, as he looked into Lisa's face.

"Leave us alone," Lisa begged, the tears rolling down her face, sobbing uncontrollably.

"I'm going to give you one more chance to be nice to me," Fred said as he wiped the tears from Lisa's eyes with his free hand.

Lisa thought she was as scared as she could be until Fred made that statement. Now, a sinking feeling

VENGEANCE IS MINE

of helplessness and hopelessness came over her as she realized what Fred intended to do

"Please, Fred," Lisa begged, "don't do this, I beg of you, please don't!"

Still holding Lisa by the hair, Fred opened the back door to John's car. Getting in first, Fred dragged Lisa in by her hair, threw her across his lap, then closed the door.

Lisa punched and scratched at Fred when she was able to regain her balance. She could feel Fred pulling at her dress and heard the sound of tearing material giving way to Fred's brutal strength.

Lisa fought a losing battle with an opponent much stronger than she was, and equally as determined. Soon Lisa's blows were reduced to not more than light slaps, as her muscles weakened from exhaustion.

Fred positioned Lisa on the back of the seat and removed what was left of her dress, stripping her down to her bra and panties. Lisa cried hysterically as all her defenses left her exhausted body.

Fred yanked at her lace bra, tearing the clasp which joined it in the front. Lisa's breasts now fully exposed, beckoned Fred to fondle and kiss them. Leaning over, Fred took one of Lisa's soft nipples into his mouth, kneading the tip with his lips, first one then the other.

By now, rage had once again built up inside of Lisa as she reached up and grabbed Fred's hair and threw him on the floorboard of the car.

Lisa sprung up and reached for the door but was grabbed by Fred on the way down. Getting off the floor, Fred slapped Lisa hard and threw her back onto the seat. Sitting on Lisa now with the full weight of his body, Fred removed his shirt, then began to open the front of his pants.

"Please stop this!" Lisa pleaded once more, but her pleas feel on deaf ears as Fred lay across her body and began caressing her with rough probing hands.

Lisa's panties tore relatively easy as Fred eliminated the last obstacle between him and his ultimate goal. Lisa was not going to make it easy for him, though, as she kept her legs firmly together.

Holding Lisa down with one had, Fred used his free hand to pry her legs apart but was unsuccessful. Getting angrier now, Fred was determined he was not going to be denied. He grabbed Lisa by the throat.

"Open your legs, bitch!" Fred ordered Lisa, but she would not comply.

Fred began to squeeze her neck a bit harder, cutting off even more of her air supply. Lisa grasped Fred's arm with both hands, struggling to free herself. She gasped for air but still defiantly refused to submit to Fred.

Fred squeezed still harder as Lisa continued to struggle more violently than before.

"Open them!" Fred yelled. "I'll let you go!"

Desperate now, Lisa had no choice, either submit or die. Lisa relaxed her leg muscles and slowly began to part them. Fred relaxed his grip on Lisa's neck just enough to allow her to breath once more, as he positioned himself between her thighs.

Releasing Lisa's neck, Fred laid on Lisa as he began the violation of her innocence.

Pain shot through Lisa's entire body as she screamed, a scream far greater than any she had screamed earlier on.

Hearing Lisa scream, Steve and Paul looked at each other and laughed.

VENGEANCE IS MINE

"Fred must really be doing some damage in there," Steve said, as he looked down at John.

Paul knelt down by John. Pulling him up by his collar, he shook John into consciousness.

"You hear that, John boy!" Paul said. "Fred's doing your woman."

Hearing Lisa yell and Paul shaking him brought John back to his faculties. Swinging hard with his left hand, John caught Paul totally by surprise, laying him out across the ground. John pounded on Paul with all the energy he could muster, ignoring the pain in his body. Paul started to get up, but John hit him again, sending him back down to the ground with a thump.

John was preparing to hit Paul again, when suddenly his breath left him, pain shooting through his body. The force of the blow sent him sprawling on the ground once again, consumed by agony.

Steve had tried to equally divide his attention between two places; listening to Lisa and Fred, as the car rocked from the activity inside, and watching Paul further torment John. Having been momentarily distracted by Lisa's screams he once again turned in the direction of John and Paul. To Steve's surprise, John had become the tormentor. He sat on Paul's chest, pelting Paul with wild swings from right to left, all landing squarely on Paul's face.

Steve planted his left foot firmly on the ground, then with his right foot kicked John squarely in the ribs with the force and technique of an extra-point kicker. John flew off Paul and landed on his back, doubled over in pain. Steve helped Paul to his feet as Paul began to once again regain his senses.

Fifteen minutes passed before Fred exited the car,

VENGEANCE IS MINE

walking over to his two buddies, he asked, "Who's next!" as he motioned to the car with his thumb.

Paul started to the car without hesitation. He entered the car and proceeded with his intended goal with far less screams and commotion than Fred had.

Each took their turn at Lisa, and each shared in the sadistic torture of John. All guilt and responsibility was equally shared.

Soon, after Steve had existed the car, Fred was ready to call it a night. He had finally taken Lisa like he was so determined to do, and he had made an example of John that all would remember if anyone tried to cross him.

Fred, Paul, and Steve walked off into the darkness, leaving the two shattered youths in their wake.

Several hours passed before Lisa was able to overcome the horror of her ordeal to function again.

Lisa sat up on the seat as pain permeated through her body, once again reminding her of her torment. She reached for the tattered remains of her clothing, attempting to clothe her bruised and shattered body.

Out the front windshield, the headlights still cast their dim white glow. Lisa was able to make out John's motionless body a short distance away in front of the car.

Lisa quickly got out of the car and ran over to John. He was lying there with one arm above his body and the other by his side. Lisa knelt beside him and once again found her tears. Thinking John was dead, she pulled at John, grabbing his arm, which lay by his side. She had little strength left as she tried again and again to roll John over. Finally, one of the attempts proved successful, and John rolled over onto his back, Lisa was horrified at the sight of his face as he rotated

VENGEANCE IS MINE

into the light of the headlights.

John's face was a bloody mess, with several large cuts above the eyes and cheekbones. His entire face was swollen by the relentless blows administered by his three assailants.

Lisa called John's name over and over again, as she tried to revive him into consciousness.

"Li-Li-sa," John said, as he tried to speak. John was only able to partially open one eye; the other was swollen shut.

"John!" Lisa said, as she looked down at him. "We've got to get you to a doctor!" She said, momentarily forgetting her pain and her need for medical attention.

"Can you help me get you to the car?" Lisa asked. John nodded his head.

Lisa pulled John by the shoulder, helping him to roll over onto his stomach. From there, John was slowly able to raise his pain-filled body to his hands and knees. With Lisa's help, John struggled to stand, staggering several times and almost sending them both back down to the ground.

Lisa placed John in the passenger side of the car and then ran around to the other side.

Turning the ignition switch, and the car's engine rolled over much too slowly to facilitate a start. Realizing the headlights must have drained the battery down, fear raced through her once again; the fear of being stuck out here with no way out. Lisa knew John needed medical attention and fast!

"God!" Lisa begged, "Help me!" Lisa turned off the headlights and sat for a moment in the total darkness the night provided. Lisa tried the car once

VENGEANCE IS MINE

more, all the while praying as she turned the key. This time, the engine sputtered with life. Her turning off the lights had given the battery just enough power to start the engine, she figured.

Lisa threw the car into reverse and backed out of the dirt road. Switching the car into drive, the tires screeched, and smoke rose as she headed into town.

VENGEANCE IS MINE

VENGEANCE IS MINE

Chapter Seven

Awoken suddenly in a cold sweat, Mrs. Duet knew something was wrong, very wrong. She rarely had these intuitions, but she had learned to trust them when she did.

Mrs. Duet paced the floor as she kept eyeing the clock on the wall, hoping her worst fears were unfounded. She called John's parents.

"Hello!" Mr. Braxton answered the phone still half asleep.

"Mr. Braxton, I'm sorry to wake you, this is Mrs. Duet."

"What can I do for you Mrs. Duet?'"

"I'm worried about the kids, Lisa has not come home yet, are they there by chance?"

"Let me check to see if the car is here." Placing the receiver on the bed, Mr. Braxton walked around the bed just as his wife was starting to sit up

"Who is it?" Mrs. Braxton asked as her husband went to the window, parted the shades, and looked out.

"It's Lisa's Mom," Mr. Braxton replied, returning to the phone.

"The car's not here," Mr. Braxton said, but before he got a response, the phone momentarily beeped, indicating another call was coming in.

"Mrs. Duet," said Mr. Braxton, "there's another call coming in, maybe it's them. I'm going to put you on hold." Mr. Braxton pressed the button to switch to the other caller.

"Hello!" said Mr. Braxton in an urgent voice.

"Mr. Braxton," the soft voice said between tears.

"Lisa, what's wrong?

"We're at the hospital," Lisa said, regaining a little of her composure.

"We'll be right there!" Mr. Braxton said, not wanting to waste any more time finding out details. All he knew was that he had to get to the hospital as fast as he could.

Mr. Braxton switched back over to Mrs. Duet. "Mrs. Duet, be ready in five minutes. We'll pick you up, John and Lisa are at the hospital. I don't know the details, but we must hurry." Mr. Braxton hung up the receiver, then turned to his closet.

Mr. Braxton was surprised to see his wife half dressed and half way out the door. She had overheard the conversation with Lisa and was wasting no time.

Mr. Braxton started his car, this one was much older than the one John had borrowed, but just as reliable.

Soon Mr. and Mrs. Braxton, along with Mrs. Duet, were speeding toward the hospital.

"Did she say what happened?" Mrs. Duet questioned Mr. Braxton as they passed through intersection after intersection; slowing down just enough to check for oncoming traffic.

"No," said Mr. Braxton, never taking his eyes off the

VENGEANCE IS MINE

road, "I didn't let her. It would have only wasted time. She'll have plenty of time to tell us when we get there."

Mr. Braxton pulled up to the front emergency entrance, and they all rushed into the hospital.

The emergency room was never an overly busy place, especially at three o'clock in the morning. But now the hospital was teaming with activity. Several police officers stood around as though waiting for instructions. Upon entering the emergency room, Mr. Braxton spotted Lisa sitting on the far side of the waiting room with three police officers. The female officer sat beside Lisa with her arm around the girl as though to comfort her. The other two officers were standing beside her, asking questions, then making notations on a small pad.

Seeing her mother, Lisa sprang up and ran toward her, throwing her arms around her mother and sobbing uncontrollably.

"What happened?" Mrs. Duet asked, having already guessed the answer by Lisa's tattered garments.

"They raped me!" Lisa said, looking down at the floor, consumed with shame.

"Mr. Braxton?" the officer asked as he walked up, taking Mr. Braxton by the shoulder. "May I speak with you, sir?" The officer pointed to another area of the hospital emergency room.

"Where's my son?" Mr. Braxton asked as he walked beside the officer, with Mrs. Braxton close behind.

"He's stable," the officer said.

"Can we see him?" Mrs. Braxton asked, anxious to see her son, to hold his hand, to know her worst fears had not come true.

"He's under sedation," the officer said, "and is being monitored, but we'll check with the doctor."

VENGEANCE IS MINE

"What happened?" Mr. Braxton demanded of the officer.

"It seems your son and his date," the officer motioned with his pad in Lisa's direction, "were out parking in the cane fields," Mr. and Mrs. Braxton were obviously shocked that John would go someplace so isolated, especially after what had happened yesterday in school.

"They were approached and assaulted by three individuals, according to the female victim."

"She has a name!" Mrs. Braxton cut in, upset by the nonchalant manner in which the deputy was explaining the sequence of events.

"Excuse me," the officer apologized. "Lisa indicated there were three attackers who took turns raping her and beating your son." The officer closed his pad and looked as though he had finished his job for the night.

"Do you have any suspects?" Mr. Braxton asked, as Mrs.
Braxton went back to Lisa, not caring to hear any more.

"We do have suspects," the officer said, "but I'm not at liberty to reveal the names at this time."

"Not at liberty!" Mr. Braxton said, starting to feel the burning anger within.

Mr. Braxton said no more as he walked back to where Lisa was.

Mrs. Duet, and his wife were sitting, one on each side of Lisa, trying to console her. Mr. Braxton sat down next to his wife just as a nurse walked up to Lisa.

"We're ready for you now," she said, then walked back to the desk and waited for her to follow. Lisa had a death grip on her mother's hand as they walked side by side, following the nurse down the hall.

Mrs. Braxton looked at Mr. Braxton after Lisa and

VENGEANCE IS MINE

her mother was out of sight. "Lisa said it was Fred, Steve, and Paul," Mrs. Braxton informed him in a scared, shaken tone. "What did the officers say?" Mrs. Braxton asked.

"He said they had suspects and that they were being picked up," said Mr. Braxton, still shaken by the identify of John's attackers.

Mr. and Mrs. Braxton waited in the lobby for another forty minutes without any word of John's status. Lisa and her mother had not yet returned, and they were growing increasingly impatient.

"Mr. and Mrs. Braxton?" A voice startled them both. They had not seen the doctor walk up, as preoccupied as they were.

"I'm Doctor Stringer, John's doctor," he introduced himself, shaking Mr. Braxton's hand and nodding to Mrs. Braxton as he sat down beside them.

"How's John?" Mr. Braxton immediately asked.

"He's going to be fine," the doctor said, trying to reassure them. "He had some internal bleeding which we stopped, a concussion, and some broken ribs."

"My God!" Mrs. Braxton said, as tears filled her eyes.

"When can we see him?" Mr. Braxton asked, also shaken by the doctor's report of John's status.

"He's heavily sedated, but I can bring you in now," the doctor said.

Mr. and Mrs. Braxton followed the doctor down the hall and into one of the rooms, opening the door and holding it for Mr. and Mrs. Braxton.

The room was relatively dark with the only light coming from a small lamp next to John's bed.

Lying motionless on the bed, his arms at his side, John had an I.V. connected to one of his arms, feeding the contents of its hanging bag into John's veins, a

VENGEANCE IS MINE

bandage wrapped around his head, along with a couple plasters taped onto his face.

His swollen and bruised face made recognition even by his mother difficult. She gasped as she realized that this was her son.

Mrs. Braxton walked to the side of John's bed, and held his hand as she wept.

"He's going to be fine," Doctor Stringer said, once again trying to reassure her.

Mr. Braxton thanked the doctor, then pulled up a chair next to John's bed and brought one for his wife.

A light tap at the door broke the silence of the room as Lisa and her mother entered.

"They won't let us stay long," Mrs. Duet said.

Upon seeing John for the first time, Mrs. Duet was taken back. "My God! What kind of animals are they?"

Lisa walked up beside Mrs. Braxton, not saying a word but just looking at John as she placed her hand on Mrs. Braxton's shoulder. Mrs. Braxton rose and hugged Lisa silently. The unspoken touch had spoken far better than words could have.

"Don't worry," Mr. Braxton said, "he's going to be all right. Now you go home and take care of yourself."

Lisa nodded, then turned to leave, taking one last look at John before she left.

Morning quickly came, and the hospital's activity had dramatically increased. Nurses came in and out on a more frequent basis, taking a wide variety of tests on John.

Mr. Braxton stretched his back.

"I'm going down to the police station," Mr. Braxton announced. His wife nodded, her head rising to give him a kiss.

Chapter Eight

Mr. Braxton left the hospital and headed straight for police headquarters, arriving at the police station just as the officers were switching shifts. Walking up to the counter, he asked the status of the arrest warrants on Fred, Paul, and Steve.

The receptionist looked bewildered as she paused for what seemed quite a while, before finally picking up the phone and pressing a series of numbers.

"Sir," she said into the receiver while looking down at the counter. "There's a gentlemen out here wanting to know the status of the arrest warrants on Steve, Paul, and Fred."

After a few moments, she returned the phone back to its cradle, then reluctantly looked at Mr. Braxton.

"Just a moment," she said, with an uneasy look on her face.

In the rear of the large office, Mr. Braxton noticed a door being quickly opened, then slammed shut, as the sheriff made his way to the counter.

"What's this crap about a warrant on my son?" The sheriff yelled as he faced Mr. Braxton from the other side of the counter.

VENGEANCE IS MINE

"I want to know when the bail hearing is," Mr. Braxton shouted back, not backing down an inch from the normally intimidating sheriff.

"What hearing?" the sheriff shouted, "What's this all about?"

"Sir," a voice from behind Mr. Braxton said, as he walked around the counter.

It was the deputy from the hospital last night, he had apparently just gotten off duty.

"I didn't want to trouble you with this last night," he said, handing the sheriff the complaint Lisa had signed some eight hours earlier.

Reading the complaint, the sheriff flew into a fit of rage.

"This is crap!" he shouted as he threw the complaint on the counter.

"Didn't you pick them up last night?" Mr. Braxton asked, directing his question to the deputy. Mr. Braxton at this point was growing increasingly more agitated as he felt his heart begin to beat faster in anger.

The deputy did not answer. He just stood there like a statue staring at Mr. Braxton.

"This is crap!" the sheriff said. "My son didn't rape or beat up anyone last night. He was at home by eleven and in his bed the rest of the night.

"Bullshit!" Mr. Braxton yelled. "And if those boys are not behind bars within the next hour, I'll have my lawyer draw up papers and sue you and this office for reckless endangerment and have your whole office investigated by the attorney general. You got an hour!" Mr. Braxton yelled. He left the office, slamming the door behind him.

VENGEANCE IS MINE

Mr. Braxton's chest burned. He hadn't realized it earlier as the pain grew stronger and stronger. Mr. Braxton stopped, learning against the wall to catch his breath. He felt his pulse. It was racing. He felt the pain spread to his neck and arm. Mr. Braxton frantically reached for his glycerin tablet, but it was too later.

"Oh my God!" were Mr. Braxton's last words as he realized the stress he had just gone through was far too much. But now it was too late. Mr. Braxton collapsed to the floor, his heart ceasing to beat even before he hit the ground.

Blurry images were all John was able to see as he began to fade in and out of consciousness. Keeping his eyes closed, John was now more conscious than not. He could hear the monitor by his bed emitting a faint, high-pitched beep every time his heart beat. John guessed he was in the hospital, or in the middle of a very bad dream. Then he realized someone was holding his hand. Feeling the sensation of touch quickly eliminated the dream theory, as he struggled once more to open his eyes.

Very blurry at first, then slowing coming into focus was his mother sitting in a chair next to his bed. She was asleep in a chair by John's bed, but had never released his hand.

John could see her now much more clearly as his eyes totally focused and he regained consciousness. John did not remember anything about what happened last night; not to mention how he had gotten in the hospital to begin with.

VENGEANCE IS MINE

John struggled to pick his brain for a clue, anything that would explain what was going on, when he heard a light tap at the door.

"Come in," John said, more out of reflex than anything else.

Upon hearing John, Mrs. Braxton woke up with delightful astonishment as she smiled into her son's face once more.

"John!" Mrs. Braxton said, still holding her son's hand, "you're going to be all right."

"What happened?" John asked, but before he was able to get an answer, the young officer who had just walked in asked if he could see Mrs. Braxton in private.

"Sure," Mrs. Braxton said, laying John's hand on the bed beside him.

John watched as his mother followed the police officer out the room.

Curiosity consumed John as he strained to hear their conversation through the curtain.

The next thing John heard was his mother scream, a scream he would remember forever.

VENGEANCE IS MINE

Chapter Nine

The same words, "No!" sounded over and over; and then all he heard was the sound of his mother crying.

John tried to get out of bed to go to his mother, but the pain was too intense; his body collapsing back in bed.

"Mama!" John yelled, hoping to get some response.

Mrs. Braxton was visibly shaken and in tears as she returned to John's bedside.

"John," she said, "I've got to go. It's your father."

"What is it?" John asked, only now realizing the man's absence.

"I'll be back as soon as I can," Mrs. Braxton said, avoiding the question.

John lay back in bed as his mother left the room. He felt helpless, unable to get out of bed. Every move caused agony.

John occupied his time staring at the ceiling, as he tried to clear the cobwebs from his head, and restore the missing pieces to the puzzle that had landed him here.

Time dragged by as John remained alone in the hospital room. The only break in the silence was an occasional round made by the nurse. Hours passed until John's mother finally did return, but she was not

VENGEANCE IS MINE

alone.   Right behind Mrs. Braxton was Father Gautreaux, the Parish Priest.

Seeing Father Gautreaux, John attempted to prolong the impending bad news by making light of the ominous situation.

"Father Gautreaux, they told me I was going to make it. No need for last rites."

The solemn expression on their faces made John realize the worst was still to come. Mrs. Braxton's blood-shot eyes told John right away she had been crying a great deal.

"John," she started, "your father is gone." She broke into uncontrollable tears once more.

Father Gautreaux went up to Mrs. Braxton and put his arm around her, trying to console her.

John realized the pain she was in, but he also felt the great void which fills a person when someone beloved dies. There were many more questions to be asked, and no matter how difficult, he was going to ask them.

"How did it happen?"

"A heart attack, they think, but we won't know for sure until the autopsy is in."

"Autopsy!" Few words sent chills through John like the word autopsy. John remembered vividly seeing a documentary on autopsy. How the body is ripped open, areas examined and weighed, and then pieced all back together again. The thought of someone doing that to his father only compounded the agony of his loss. John put his arm around his mother as she sat on the edge of the bed with her head lowered and weeping. Pulling his mom toward him, he embraced her, sharing their agony as they wept together for the first time.

VENGEANCE IS MINE

John was released from the hospital just in time for his father's funeral. He regretted not being able to be of any help to his mom for the many arrangements she had to make. But the good news was that he was released from confinement. The stay in the hospital had seemed a lot longer than it was. There were no visitors, his mother was busy making funeral arrangements, and Lisa had not called or come by to visit. John's head was clear now, clear about everything except what had happened that night. He remembered going to the movie with Lisa, but the next memory was that of the hospital emergency room.

Mrs. Braxton pulled up to the front door of the hospital just as John was being rolled out in a wheelchair.

"Thank you," John said. He got up reaching for the car door, anxious to put this experience behind him.

"You're most welcome, sir," the orderly said, as he spun the wheelchair about and headed back into the hospital.

"Hi Mom," John said, settling into the car.

Mrs. Braxton was dressed completely in black in a dress, hat, and veil.

"The suit looks good on you," Mrs. Braxton replied, commenting on the suit she had sent him to wear. John only had one suit, and it wasn't black. Mrs. Braxton had gone out and bought him one, having it altered to his size.

"Thank you," John replied, not losing sight of the reason the suit was bought.

The funeral was to be a simple one, following his father's request, which he had often made after attending funerals of relatives and friends. Mr. Braxton felt the hours of lying in wait were just too hard on all

VENGEANCE IS MINE

concerned. Mr. Braxton wanted a simple ceremony at the graveside conducted by Father Gautreaux.

When John and his mother arrived, a small crowd had gathered to pay their last respects to Mr. Braxton. The priest and hearse had also arrived, but Mr. Braxton's coffin had remained in the hearse until Mrs. Braxton arrived.

John and his mother took their places by Father Gautreaux as the coffin was removed from the hearse and slowly carried by the pallbearers. The coffin was placed over the grave, held in place by the nylon lowering straps. Attendants then placed flowers on top as Father Gaurtreaux began his service.

"It's funny the little things you remember," John thought as the priest's sermon faded to the background of his mind. Staring at the coffin, John remembered his father. He remembered the trips they went on together, hunting and fishing. He remembered how his dad had always made time for him when he needed his advice. But most of all, he remembered how hard his dad had worked to provide a living for him and his mother, never once complaining of the weight of the burden or the depth of the sacrifice. John looked up for a moment and spotted Lisa. This was the first time he had seen her since the "incident". Lisa stared at John with a piercing stare and a hardened look John had never seen before.

John looked away from Lisa, trying not to get too far removed from the proceedings. He would have to deal with this in time.

Father Gautreaux was ending his sermon as John reached down and picked up a handful of dirt and tossed it on his father's coffin.

VENGEANCE IS MINE

The crowd each passed by and offered John and his mother their sympathy.

Lisa and her mother were the last to come to them. Lisa looked straight at John.

"Can I speak to you for a moment?" she said, then walked a distance away, turning to see if John was following.

John followed Lisa to a spot about twenty-five yards away from their mothers.

"Lisa," John started, "why didn't you come see me in the hospital?"

"I had my own problems to deal with!" Lisa said, in as harsh a tone as John had ever heard. There was something very wrong with Lisa, a bitter girl now, as she started her questioning of John.

"What's this I hear about your memory?" she asked in a demanding tone.

"It's true, I have certain areas which are blacked out," John explained.

"And about that night?" Lisa questioned.

"I can't remember a thing," John said.

"You bastard!" Lisa screamed. "I was raped by three of those bastards, and you can't remember!"

Lisa chose to have her suffering overshadow any other. Even John's bruised face did not once bring her to feel for anyone but herself.

"Well, Johnny boy, we go to court in a week. I hope your memory is back by then because I'm not facing them alone." With that, Lisa started to walk away. John reached for her arm, wanting to say more, anything to bring back the old Lisa.

"Don't touch me!" Lisa screamed. "Don't ever touch me!" John pulled back, and Lisa walked back to her mother.

VENGEANCE IS MINE

Lisa's mother met her half way, and they stopped for a moment as Lisa said something to her mother. Then Lisa walked back to their car alone while her mother walked to John.

"John," Mrs. Duet started, "forgive Lisa. She's been through a lot. She's on the verge of hysteria. She wanted to know if you're going to be on her side at the trial."

"You know I will, Mrs. Duet."

"That's good to know, John. If your facts are little hazy, maybe we can get together and go over them?"

"You're going to tell me the story you want me to recite in court?"

"No, John, not like that, just try to help you remember the facts."

"The fact is I can't remember."

"NO!" said Mrs. Duet in a much stronger tone. "The facts are three animals raped my baby and nearly killed you. And if you don't testify, it'll be Lisa's word against all three of them, not to mention the money and influence their fathers will throw into it.

"I know it's hard to think straight right now, but when you get it together, come to the house. We'll help each other." Saying that, Mrs. Duet did not wait for a reply. She turned and walked to her car where Lisa waited.

"What was all that about?" John's mother asked, curious to know the gist of the conversation.

"They want to make sure I have my story right when I go to court."

"Well! Do you?" she asked.

"Mom, you know I can't remember a thing."

"John, Lisa knows who they are, and in time your memory will come back and you will remember too. But

VENGEANCE IS MINE

when it does, it may be too late to punish the boys who perpetuated this awful attack on ya'll. Bending the truth may be the only way to guarantee justice."

John listened to his mother and to the case she made for him to perjure himself on the stand. After thinking through every option, he decided to do it.

Upon reaching home, John went immediately to the phone where he called Lisa, anxious to share with her his decision. Mrs. Duet answered the phone, "Hello, Mrs. Duet, is Lisa there?"

"She's lying down. -- John?"

"Yes, ma'am, I've decided to take you up on your offer."

"That's great to hear. Lisa will be pleased. John, let's plan for three o'clock tomorrow afternoon."

"That will be fine," John agreed.

John looked forward to seeing Lisa again. The brief encounter they had had earlier in the day had left John with a sad and empty feeling. His heart grew heavy at the thought of them drifting apart. He was determined to find a way to reconcile with her, to get some sort of normalcy back in their shattered lives. But John didn't know if Lisa felt the same way or not All he knew was that he would do everything in his power to make it right.

VENGEANCE IS MINE

VENGEANCE IS MINE

Chapter Ten

The following afternoon, John headed over to Lisa's house. Knocking on the door, he was immediately greeted by Mrs. Duet.

"Come in, John," she said, motioning to the living room. "Lisa will be down shortly."

John sat in the living room, trying to recall anything that would contribute to the prosecution of Fred, Paul and Steve. All John knew was what his mother had told him. He and Lisa had gone parking down a dirt road in the cane fields. Then Steve, Fred, and Paul arrived, dragged him from his car, beat him, then raped Lisa. John thought the case would be an easy one, regardless of his memory loss. But this was Houma, a town controlled by a few powerful people who could administer justice the way they saw fit.

Lisa entered the living room with her mother right behind her. John could not help but notice her bedraggled appearance. Lisa wore blue jeans, no shoes, and a gray sweatshirt. Her long blond hair was pulled back in a pony tail, that only highlighted her lack of makeup and blood-shot eyes.

Lisa sat in a single armchair a short distance from John, while Mrs. Duet sat next to John on the couch.

VENGEANCE IS MINE

"John, Mrs. Duet started, "as you know, we are dealing with some powerful people. The parents of the boys who harmed ya'll that is. I've spoken to the D.A., but he will not be trying the case. He has too many other cases on backlog to give our case priority. An Assistant District Attorney will handle the case. It smells like corrupt manipulation of the legal system to me. This is why we must be firm in our conviction! Steve's parents have hired a lawyer out of New York to handle the defense and he is supposedly the best in the country.

"John," Mrs. Duet continued, "they will do everything they can to discredit you and Lisa. But if you and Lisa stand together, we can win."

John looked over to Lisa, who had remained silent, through most of the conversation. Her hardened, piercing eyes still stabbed him.

"John," Mrs. Duet continued, "I think all we should have to do is to identify the boys and acknowledge the fact that they were indeed the ones who attached you. If that happens, no local jury could return anything less than a guilty verdict. The townspeople all know what the boys are like. Very few of them remain untouched by the bullies in one way or another."

"We'll get a conviction," John said in a reassuring tone.

As John rose, he turned once more to Lisa.

"Lisa," John said in a soft voice. "May I speak with you?"

Lisa never looked at John. She got up, and as she was leaving, said, "We have nothing to talk about."

John was hurt far more than any beating could have hurt him. He felt the only woman he had ever loved slipping away from him.

VENGEANCE IS MINE

Lisa's mother placed her hand on John's shoulder in an attempt to console him. "She'll come around, John. Just be patient."

John shook his head half-heartedly, hoping she was right. But he had an uneasy feeling that she was completely wrong.

"Thank you, Mrs. Duet," John said, as he opened the door. "I'll see you next week in court."

A week can be the longest seven days in a person's life when he is waiting for legal proceedings to arrive. The week had been passing slowly though uneventfully until about mid-week. John and his mother received a phone call from the District Attorney's office. Mrs. Braxton had assumed it was about the trial against Fred and his two partners in crime. She was shocked to realize it was about criminal proceeding against John for his altercation with Fred at the high school.

"Three days!" John heard Mrs. Braxton say. "It's not enough time!" She pleaded but to no avail.

Hanging up the phone, Mrs. Braxton turned to John. "John, a trial date has been set on the 15th, the same day as the other trial and to be heard by the same judge. Judge Parker!"

"Oh, my God!' John said, realizing the significance of the judge's selection.

"Steve's and Fred's father put him in office!" John said, realizing how the trial was being stacked against him.

"Don't worry, John," Mrs. Braxton said, trying to reassure her son. "I'll get in touch with Mr. Morrison. He'll know what to do," Mrs. Braxton once again picked up the phone and dialed Mr. Morrison's office.

"Good morning, Mr. Morrison's office. How can I help you?" asked a young, pleasant voice.

VENGEANCE IS MINE

"This is Mrs. Braxton. I need to speak to Mr. Morrison."

"I'm sorry, Mr. Morrison is on vacation and can't be reached."

"How long is he going to be on vacation?" asked Mrs. Braxton, pushing for more information.

"Two weeks," responded the secretary.

"Is there no way he can be reached?" asked Mr. Braxton.

"No, ma'am, he's on a hunting trip in Mexico, and there is no way to contact him."

"Well, if he should happen to call in, tell him I need to talk to him. It's an emergency!"

When she hung up, Mrs. Braxton immediately reached for the phone book, turning to the yellow pages until she came to "attorney". This is very fishy," she said, talking to herself.

She began dialing attorneys, going down the list in the yellow pages. It didn't take her long to realize a pattern was forming.

Each time she called, she was greeted with polite helpful consideration until she gave her name. She was then immediately told that the attorney for which the secretary worked was booked up. Each law office was the same. Word had gotten out that John's case was poison, and no one would take it.

Mrs. Braxton was at a loss; her son was about to be tried, and she couldn't get a lawyer to represent him. She knew her only chance was to seek help outside the parish.

Grabbing the car keys and purse, Mrs. Braxton started toward the door.

VENGEANCE IS MINE

"I've got to run some errands," she called to John as she was closing the door behind her. She didn't want to worry him about the dilemma she found herself in.

Mrs. Braxton realized she would have to go out of the parish if she was to get any help for John. Then it came to her. The name of an attorney who could possibly help.

VENGEANCE IS MINE

VENGEANCE IS MINE

Chapter Eleven

Claude Boudreaux had at one time been a promising young attorney until he fell out of favor with the powers that be in Houma. He lived now in Thibodeaux, Louisiana, located in the neighboring parish of Lafourche, about a thirty-minute ride from Houma.

Mrs. Braxton arrived in town at about two o'clock and went directly to Main Street. Parking was difficult downtown, and Mrs. Braxton had to circle the block several times before finding a spot.

Putting money in the meter, Mrs. Braxton hurried to locate the law office of Claude Boudreaux. Mr. Boudreaux had been a practicing attorney in Houma, but after an attempt to unseat a corrupt parish judge, his life had taken a drastic and unforeseen turn.

The local judge had been a confidante of the few power brokers who actually ran the parish, and there was no way they were going to lose him.

A smear campaign was launched which cast doubt on Mr. Boudreaux's character. The campaign was so massive and subtle that he lacked the means to launch an effective defense.

The final analysis was that his reputation had been ruined by unsubstantiated and malicious allegations

VENGEANCE IS MINE

which were never proven, but which succeeded in destroying his practice. Having few options at this point, Mr. Boudreaux chose to leave the parish he loved and relocated to Thibodeaux to rebuilt what was left of his career.

Mrs. Braxton had not walked far when she saw the sign on the wall:

Law Office Of Claude Boudreaux

There was nothing fancy about the building. It surely was not located in a high rent district.

Mrs. Braxton pulled on the oak door, attempting to gain access to the building. As she pulled, the top of the door was the only part that would budge. The bottom of the door was stuck. Finally, after much effort, the door opened and Mrs. Braxton entered the office.

Inside sat a middle-aged woman behind a desk, doing her nails.

"May I help you?" she asked, looking up from her nails.

"Yes, is Mr. Boudreaux in?"

"Yes, replied the receptionist, "go right in."

Looking up from his work, he greeted Mrs. Braxton with a disarming smile.

"Hello, Mr. Boudreaux," Mrs. Braxton said. "My name is Mrs. Braxton, and I need your help."

Mr. Boudreaux stood up when Mrs. Braxton entered, and motioned her to sit down in one of the chairs in front of his desk.

Mr. Boudreaux was younger than she had remembered him, probably in his mid-thirties, she guessed. His balding forehead was the only telltale sign.

"What seems to be the problem?"

VENGEANCE IS MINE

"My son is in trouble, and I am unable to find an attorney to help him."

"What did you son do, Mrs. Braxton?"

"He defended himself when a boy came at him with a knife!"

"Well, it doesn't sound like a difficult case," Mr. Boudreaux surmised.

"Mr. Boudreaux, I'll be honest with you. The reason I came to you is that I'm from Houma and I knew you once practiced there and are aware of the peer structure that exists. I feel my son will be railroaded if I can't get him help." At this point her desperation became apparent, not only in her voice but also in her visual expressions.

"Whom did your son defend himself against?" Mr. Boudreaux questioned.

"Fred Smith," Mrs. Braxton explained.

"Is he any relation to Sheriff Smith?" Mr. Boudreaux asked, waiting for a response.

"He's his father!"

Mr. Boudreaux turned his chair slightly to the side, then leaned back and stared at the wall.

"Mrs. Braxton, your son is in a great deal of trouble. As you know, I once lived in Houma until Mr. Smith decided to run me out. He is an extremely powerful man, and most importantly, he has powerful friends."

Mrs. Braxton could sense the anxiety in Mr. Boudreaux. His calm, carefree manner had taken a dramatic shift. He seemed more intense now, more focused.

"For me to go back would only be inviting trouble."

"Please!" Mrs. Braxton pleaded. "You're my only hope."

VENGEANCE IS MINE

Mr. Boudreaux knew the anger, frustration, and sense of hopelessness Mrs. Braxton felt. It wasn't too long ago he had experienced the same feelings ultimately inflicted by the same people.

"Mrs. Braxton, you realize that there may not be a whole lot I can do to help your son. In fact, I might ultimately do him more harm."

"You're my only chance. No other lawyer will even talk to me."

"Very well, Mrs. Braxton. Leave a five hundred dollars retainer with my secretary, and I'll do what I can."

"Thank you, Mr. Boudreaux. Thank you!" Mrs. Braxton said, then left his office, stopping at the secretary's desk to pay the retainer.

Mr. Boudreaux sat at his desk and pondered his chances of getting Mrs. Braxton's son off. He calculated the chances to be slim to none. But he was going to try, despite not feeling very good about the whole situation. He realized the deck was stacked against him, and the outcome had already been determined.

The drive back seemed to have taken twice as long as it had to get to Thibodeaux. Driving down the country road, thoughts bounced around Mrs. Braxton's mind as she headed toward Houma. She thought of her husband and how he would have handled this insurmountable impasse that faced her. She could only hope she was doing the right thing.

As she entered the driveway, John came out to meet her, greeting her with a small kiss on the cheek.

"Good news, John! We have an attorney."

"Great!" John said. "Who? How?"

"Mr. Boudreaux out of Thibodeaux."

VENGEANCE IS MINE

"What!" John exclaimed, knowing the rumors that had been spread about the man. "I didn't know he was still practicing."

"Well, he is, John, and regardless of what you have heard, we have to trust him. He is the only one who is willing to help us."

John had to agree with his mother.

Mr. Boudreaux moved quickly. He called John and his mother to explain the game plan.

Mr. Boudreaux was going to submit several pretrial motions in which he would ask to have the trial moved out of the parish. If that failed, he was going to request that the scheduled judge to preside over the hearing recluse himself. Mr. Boudreaux knew him too well, knew his ties to the boys' families and knew what verdict he would return.

Unsuccessfully in each of his attempts, Mr. Boudreaux finally leveled with Mrs. Braxton and John. "We need to keep hoping for the best," he assured them. "I will not desert you, but you need to brace yourself for the worst."

The day in question soon arrived. It had the bittersweet feeling of an unwelcome guest. But it had to be faced, and John and his mother would face it together.

The courtroom was nearly empty as John, his mother, and Mr. Boudreaux walked into the room. The only people present were Fred, Paul, and Steve, their families, and lawyers. All sat behind the defendants.

Lisa sat next to the prosecutor, staring straight ahead. Her mother sat directly behind her.

Only a few other people were in the courtroom. There were people who had nothing to do with the case

VENGEANCE IS MINE

and could not care less about the outcome. They viewed court proceedings as a source of entertainment.

As John and his mother walked down the aisle, John avoided looking in the trio's direction. He could feel their stares however, piercing through him like a hot knife through butter.

John had not spoken to, or seen Lisa or her mother since their meeting a week earlier. With all the pretrial motions and meeting with the attorney, John had little time left by the end of the day. Lisa and John's eyes made contact briefly as he took his seat behind the prosecution's table.

Lisa and John did not speak, nor did their mothers. They sat patiently waiting for the judge to appear. They watched as the young Assistant District Attorney organized his papers for the case.

The A.D.A. rose and approached John, Lisa and their mothers.

"I'm afraid I have some bad news," he said. "I called this morning to get confirmation on the DNA test. It seems all the samples have been lost."

"Lost!" John exclaimed. What do you mean lost?"

"Just that," the A.D.A. continued, "and without the DNA reports, I have a very weak case. I just wanted to let you know."

Thoughts raced through their minds. Were the missing samples just the first step in a long spiral downward?

As the judge entered, the resounding voice of the bailiff boomed, "All Rise!"

Everyone in the courtroom stood up, then took their seats and waited for "justice".

The trial proceeded at a brisk pace as the defense attorney made motion after motion, which were

VENGEANCE IS MINE

countered by the prosecutor. It did not take John, nor anyone else, long to realize that the young prosecuting attorney was outgunned by the high-powered defense attorney. After several more motions, mostly insignificant, the judge finally dropped his bombshell. The judge sedately announced that he would decide the case rather than have a jury convene. Vigorously objecting, the A.D.A. was soon put in his place by the judge.

"The defendants are the ones who have the option of a trial by jury. They also have the option of the judge deciding the case. Now, Sir, I would hate to think that the only reason you want a jury trial is that you question my integrity."

"No, Your Honor, but ...

"No buts. I've said how it is going to be. Now call your first witness."

John and Lisa were shocked. They wondered what kind of trail was this going to be.

"Your Honor, I'd like to call Lisa Duet to the witness stand."

Lisa rose from her seat and headed toward the witness stand.

The bailiff walked up to her with a rather oversized Bible and asked her to raise her right hand and place her left one on the Bible.

"Do you swear to tell the truth, the whole, truth, and nothing but the truth, so help you God."

"I do," Lisa responded.

It was only at this point that Lisa noticed a face from her past.

Seated in the middle of the courtroom was Lisa's former boyfriend from New Orleans. Lisa was shocked as she stared at him. He had a helpless look on his face

VENGEANCE IS MINE

as he held up a subpoena, indicating to Lisa he had no choice in being there.

The defense had spared no expense and had left no rock unturned. Lisa could only wait and hope for the best.

"Miss Duet," the A.D.A. started, "would you tell us what happened on the night of May 19th?"

Lisa, visibly nervous, began to recite the events in a shaky voice.

"My boyfriend and I were out on a date. We had gone to a movie, then to eat. After leaving the restaurant, we drove a little way out of town to look at the stars. That's when those three animals came up --"

"Objection, Your Honor!" the defense attorney immediately jumped in.

"Sustained," the judge said, as he turned to Lisa.

"Young lady, you will keep your remarks strictly to the facts!"

"Yes, sir," Lisa said.

"Continue, Lisa," the prosecution coaxed her.

"Well, we were sitting in the car when the glass on the driver side window shattered and John was pulled out of the car."

"Then what happened?"

"They beat John and beat him until he was unconscious."

"They - you mean the defendants?" asked the attorney.

"Yes," said Lisa.

"Go on."

Lisa hung her head as she was overcome by shame sitting before the three boys who had violated her. But through her tears, she managed to continue.

VENGEANCE IS MINE

"They took turns raping me," Lisa said, sobbing uncontrollably by now.

"Do you see the boys that raped you in this courtroom?"

"Yes."

"Will you point them out to the court."

Lisa looked up at the boys for the first time since the assault. With a trembling hand, she pointed to the trio. "That's them -- Fred, Paul, and Steve."

"Thank you, Lisa." Turning to the defense attorney, he said, "Your witness."

The defense attorney remained seated for a while, then rose and approached Lisa.

"Miss Duet," the attorney asked, "do you go parking in remote areas very often?" He stood before the witness box with one hand on the rail and the other in his pocket.

"No!" Lisa responded coldly.

"Was this your first time?"

"Objection, Your Honor. This line of questioning has no bearing on what happened that night. Whether Miss Duet has ever been parking or not is totally irrelevant."

"Overruled!" The Judge barked his ruling, sending the prosecutor in retreat.

"Answer the question," the judge directed Lisa.

"No," Lisa replied.

This response had not only caught John by surprise but Lisa's mother also.

"Is it safe to say you had been more than twice?"

Lisa hesitated, reluctant to answer.

"May I remind you that you are still under oath."

Lisa looked out on the courtroom, knowing her former boyfriend would be called up next. Lisa felt helpless.

VENGEANCE IS MINE

Her only choice was to tell the truth. No matter whom it hurt.

"Yes," Lisa finally replied, "more than twice."

"So it is safe to say you've been several times."

"Yes," replied Lisa reluctantly.

"Your parking area, at the time of the attack, was it by a main highway?"

"Yes, we were by Highway 90."

"Miss Duet, how long have you known the defendants?"

"A year, I guess. I've just seen them around school."

"Before your attack, did you ever have any cross words with the defendants?"

"No!"

"Did the defendants at any time try to force themselves on you?"

"No, but --"

"Just answer the question; yes or no. Miss Duet, isn't it true you made it a daily habit of going out of your way to talk to the defendants, almost to a point of becoming a nuisance?"

"That's a lie!" Lisa shouted.

"Miss Duet, I don't doubt for one minute that you and your boyfriend were attacked.

But Miss Duet, you are lying when you say in sworn testimony that my clients perpetuated this crime."

"No!"

"Yes, isn't this part of a plan that you and your boyfriend cooked up to discredit my clients in another case pending before this court where your boyfriend faces possible jail time?"

"No!" Lisa exclaimed, trying to break the momentum of the defense attorney.

VENGEANCE IS MINE

"Lisa, isn't it true that you and your boyfriend were beat up by transients and that you and he took advantage of the situation to implicate my clients?"

"That's not true!" Lisa pleaded.

"No further question, Your Honor."

With that, Lisa left the witness stand and returned to her seat with her mother.

The prosecutor rose once more.

"Your Honor, I would like to call to the stand John Braxton."

After being sworn in, John took the stand.

"Mr. Braxton, do you have anything to add to the testimony Miss Duet just gave?"

"No, sir, it happened just like she said it did."

"And do you see the men who attacked you in this courtroom?"

"Yes, Sir, that's them!"

"Let the record show the witnesses indicated the defendants. That's all, Your Honor."

The defense attorney walked over to John and leaned on the rail of the witness box.

"Mr. Braxton, the prosecution states you were beaten pretty badly that night."

"Yes, I was."

"How clearly do you remember the events of that night?"

"Very clearly," John said with conviction and confidence.

"Lisa has testified that you went to a movie and then dinner."

"That's right," John confirmed.

"What did you eat?"

VENGEANCE IS MINE

"Objection, Your Honor!" The young A.D.A. sprang to his feet. "This line of questioning is totally irrelevant."

"Your Honor," the defense replied, "this has to do with the client's memory. When the plaintiff was brought to the hospital, he experienced a memory loss. I'm only trying to establish the extent to which his memory has recovered."

The judge paused only briefly, then indicated his decision.

"Overruled!"

John paused, caught completely off guard by this question. Reflecting back to Lisa's house where they had supposedly gotten their facts straight about the attack, down to the last detail, but they had forgotten about the rest of the night. John strained to think, to recall this bit of information which his memory refused to release for some reason.

John remained silent for some time until the defense attorney spoke again.

"Well, John, that might be a little tough. Tell me John, where did you go to eat with Lisa?"

John once again paused, unable to answer his question.

"Can you remember the movie you saw? Yes or no, John."

Pausing for a while longer, John finally spoke.

"No, sir."

"You can't remember the very first events of that night, but yet you are able to describe the series of events which occurred when you got assaulted. John, you need to come clean and come clean now. Remember, John, you are under oath. Also remember the penalties for perjury.

VENGEANCE IS MINE

"Now I'll ask you, can you positively and absolutely say that these three boys were the ones that attacked you that night?"

John paused a long while before answering the question, hoping the question might somehow go away. But, it didn't.

The attorney asked the question once more.

"John, I need your answer."

"No!" John reluctantly submitted, breaking down and offering the response the attorney wanted.

"No further questions, your Honor."

As John left the bench, he saw the look on Lisa's face. He saw there a look of total betrayal, as though he had single-handedly set the boys free.

"Your Honor." The defense attorney stood before the judge as he addressed him. "At this time I would like to move for a dismissal."

"On what grounds, Counselor?" the judge asked more as a matter of procedure than an actual question.

"Your Honor, we have heard a case which has been totally fabricated from the start. There is no evidence to put my clients at the scene. The alleged victim did have sex that night in question, but there is no way to determine if it was before or after the beating of her boyfriend. Any testing which could have been done on the semen samples is no longer possible. The prosecution seems to have misplaced his evidence. Yet he seeks to prosecute this case on unsubstantiated testimony and even worse, on perjured testimony. We do concede the fact that John Braxton was beaten by a person or person, making the events of that night unclear to him. But for him to come into court and perjure himself with an obviously rehearsed testimony is unconscionable.

VENGEANCE IS MINE

"It is still unclear what Miss Duet's motive is for accusing my clients of this hideous crime. Did she think the opportunity presented itself as one in which she thought she could help her boyfriend with his other legal problems, as well as seek vengeance on the boys who rejected her advances? We don't know, Your Honor. But in her own testimony, Miss Duet admitted to frequenting cane fields for the purpose of sex."

"Objection, Your Honor," the prosecution interjected but was quickly overruled by the judge.

"What we have here, Your Honor, is an emotionally disturbed girl who had been rejected by my three clients when she tried to sway them with her female charms. Hell hath no fury like a woman scorned, and that is exactly what we have here, Your Honor." The defense attorney concluded his argument then returned to his seat.

Lisa sat sobbing as she listened to the defense attorney. Lisa leaned over at one point, pleading to the prosecution to stop him.

"He's making me out to be a crazy whore!" Lisa wept. But the prosecutor was only able to interject one objection. He had known his case had been very weak going in. The strongest part of the whole case was the testimony of John and Lisa. When John's testimony had been proven to be a rehearsed fabrication of someone else's recollection, he saw the case slipping away.

Judge Parker paused for a moment, then looking over to the prosecution, he asked, "Do you have any more evidence for this case?"

The beaten prosecutor could offer none, simply saying, "Your Honor, I do not."

VENGEANCE IS MINE

"This case has been a tragedy in many ways," the Judge started as he prepared to render his verdict. "But the most tragic is when three fine youths' reputation can be dragged through the mud by individuals with questionable morals. This case should have never been brought to trial. The only evidence that could have exonerated the accused was either destroyed or lost. The court system is based on facts, and the prosecution has failed to present its case." Pausing momentarily, the judge continued, "I therefore find the accused innocent and they are free to go."

Anger raged inside of Lisa as she saw the direction the judge was heading. Gradually and steadily, like a volcano building up pressure before it finally erupts, Lisa remained silent until the judge rendered his verdict. Then she screamed an ear-piercing shriek. "No!" You can't let them go. They raped me!" Lisa was uncontrollable as she took on the appearance of a crazed animal, having to be restrained by her mother.

"You animals," she yelled, turning away from the judge to the three accused. She next charged at the three boys. Reason was no longer a part of Lisa. She was now driven by rage and hate.

John grabbed Lisa before she could reach the other side of the courtroom.

Using all her strength, Lisa swung wildly at John.

"It's your fault," she yelled as she tried to score blows to John's face.

Lisa was quickly subdued by the bailiff and was led off screaming.

When Lisa was taken away, her mother also left. Unable to go with her daughter, she exited the court from the rear, not saying a word to John or his mother as she left. Very in control, never making eye contact,

VENGEANCE IS MINE

Mrs. Duet had also been shocked by the verdict. She realized that there was nothing else that could have been said that would have changed the verdict.

John looked to his left. There Fred, Paul, and Steve were being smothered with hugs and handshakes. After the celebration, the group slowly headed out of the courtroom.

Fred's eyes met John's as he smirked.

Words alone could never describe the way John felt. It was as though his whole life had been cast into the abyss with no way for him to regain control of it.

Mr. Boudreaux leaned over to John, taking him by the shoulder, "We're next on the docket," he said, and they walked to the defense table in front of the court. They were going from one side of the court to the other.

About that time, the D.A. entered the room. Although John had never met the man, he recognized him from his campaign posters. John was immediately struck by the fact that an assistant was to try the rape and assault trial, yet the D. A. himself was going to try John's case.

"John," Mr. Bordeaux said, "I'm afraid I have some more bad news for you. We were unable to subpoena any witnesses. The trial was scheduled so quickly, and the timing couldn't be worse. Almost everybody is away on some sort of end-of-school blowout in Florida."

John shook his head in understanding. If there was one thing John didn't need, it was to be reminded how bad things were.

Judge Parker entered the courtroom once more, observing the usual formalities as before.

John's case proceeded with a much more orchestrated and organized performance from the D. A.

VENGEANCE IS MINE

Most of the proceedings were a blur to John, until the very end, when the judge pronounced his verdict.

"Will the defendant please rise," the bailiff ordered.

"Young man," Judge Parker said, "your acts were callous in nature, and although the results were not fatal, they most assuredly could have been. It is my obligation to protect the community from individuals such as yourself who pose a threat to society. Therefore, it is the decision of this court that you be sentenced to the State correction facility at Angola for a period of ten years without parole, for assault with the intent to commit murder."

John was in a state of shock. He could not believe the system could be so corrupt, so crooked that it would destroy his life when his only crime was defending himself from a crazed lunatic.

John could hear his attorney making objections and motions. He could feel his crying mother being pried away from him as she struggled to get one last embrace before he was taken away.

To John, though, it was as though everything around him had slowed down and become distorted. His mind was dazed by the verdict as though he had been physically struck.

As John was led off by the bailiff, he could hear his mother promising to appeal the case and to get him out.

VENGEANCE IS MINE

VENGEANCE IS MINE

Chapter Twelve

John woke from his memories as a heavy metal key shifted the bolt to his cell door.

"Get up, John, it's time to go!" the guard ordered; positioning himself outside the cell door, waiting to escort him.

As John gathered his few belongings, he reflected back to when he had first arrived. For years, he had only one goal in mind, to devise a painful and brutal death for each of the conspirators who had landed him in this hellhole. Paul, Fred, and Steve would be made to pay and made to pay in a big way. This had been his only reason to survive this torture. Lisa's suicide shortly after he had been incarcerated had only made him more focused, more determined. Fred, Steve, and Paul had killed Lisa, they had killed her just as surely as if they had sliced her wrist with their own hands.

Lisa had gone into a deep depression after the trial, never leaving her room, until her mother came home one day and found her dead. John's mother had broken the news to him on one of her monthly visits.

They said time heals all wounds, but some wounds just couldn't be healed. Only the demise of the victim or the victims can repair the festering wound which time inevitable worsens.

VENGEANCE IS MINE

John's memory had suppressed some of the details of what had happened ten years ago, but the invitation somehow refreshed and revived his memory, causing him to recall in great detail a time and a place ten years earlier. A memory that had remained in the recesses of his mind for years now began resurrecting itself in quick flashes at first but then moving stronger and steadier. Glass shattering, pain, more pain than he had ever experienced in his life. These glimpses continued to linger until John had a complete mental picture of the events that had happened that night.

John thought about how strange it all was. For years, he had tried to recall certain events of that night, without success. Finally, John had given up and blocked it all from his mind.

The invitation had somehow brought it all back.

As John and the guard walked past cell after cell, John said goodbye to some of the men that had befriended him since his arrival. John knew if it had not been for them, a young boy wouldn't stand much of a chance staying alive and unmolested in a cesspool like this.

Each area John passed brought back a bad memory of some sort. For ten years, John had made this place home. Leaving now seemed somehow unreal. He kept waiting for something to happen, waiting for someone to say they had made an error and that his time had not yet been fully served. He thought of the possibility of additional time for one of the many fights he had been involved in, an oversight that would not be realized until just before his release. He held the excitement of being released closely in check in case of such a possibility.

Through gate after gate, guard after guard, they progressed toward the processing station. This was

VENGEANCE IS MINE

without a doubt the longest walk John had ever taken, not because of the uncertainty, but because of the persistent vision in John's head of being stopped before his final release. This made each step, and each second seem exaggerated both in time and distance.

Finally arriving at the processing station, the guard returned to John the few valuables he had entered prison with: a watch that had long since stopped, a high school ring that no longer fit, and a wallet that contained identification which had expired ten years earlier.

As the steel door opened, John finally stood before the last portal between him and freedom.

"Good luck," the guard said, with no real conviction. It had become habit for him to say it.

Without delay, John walked through the door, not bothering to respond to the guard. For the first time in ten years, John stood on ground where he was free. As a free man, he breathed air that wasn't tainted by the smell of prison. For the first time in years, John felt good again.

John's mother was waiting as he came out the door. The excitement she felt was almost indescribable. For the first time in ten years, she would be able to touch her son, to kiss his cheek, and to hug his neck. The restrictions placed on visitations had never allowed this, and she had so missed it. Mrs. Braxton had visited John faithfully, and from the start, she had begun to notice the change in John. She was getting to see first-hand how a sweet, loving boy could be transformed into a cold, emotionless man.

"John!" Mrs. Braxton called as she ran toward him and hugged him hard and long, as though in an

VENGEANCE IS MINE

attempt to somehow regain ten years worth of hugs in a few seconds.

"It's great to be out!" John told his mother as she finally released him from her vice-like embrace.

"Well, Mrs. Braxton, you think you can find work for an ex-con?" John asked his mother as they walked back to the car.

Since John's conviction, Mrs. Braxton had tried month after month to get John's conviction overturned, or at least reduced, but the judge had been shrewd and calculating in the wording of the verdict. Each attempted appeal or verdict reduction was dismissed.

The expenses of attorneys and court costs had quickly used up all of her husband's life insurance money, thus leaving her no choice but to reopen her husband's hardware store. At first, she had found it extremely difficult, but the local townspeople were very supportive, and she learned as she went. Mrs. Braxton, for never having worked outside the home, proved to be a savvy businesswoman. In no time at all, she had not only recaptured lost business but had also started to increase it. Mrs. Braxton could have sold the store, and if managed properly, the money received from the sale would have been more than enough to support herself. Mrs. Braxton knew, however, that her son would need a way to support himself once he got out. Ex-cons were normally not the first people potential employers sought out for career opportunities. So what John had resisted for so many years would prove to be his salvation. He would do what his father had hoped and take over the business.

All the way back to town, John and his mother only engaged in casual chitchat. Nothing of any importance was mentioned until they approached the cemetery.

VENGEANCE IS MINE

"I'd like to stop if you don't mind," John asked.

"Sure, honey, we'll stop."

After making several turns on the curvy drive, Mrs. Braxton finally brought the car to a stop near a large oak tree. John recognized it as the area where his dad was buried. Getting out of the car, John walked over to his dad's headstone, not needing direction, even though the small cemetery had filled up a lot in ten years.

John knelt by his father's headstone while his mother stood a short distance away, allowing him a little privacy. John could clearly picture his dad behind the hardware counter making jokes and talking to his customers. Even time had not blurred that image.

After several minutes, John rose and walked over to his mother.

"Where did they place Lisa?" John asked.

"Over there," she said softly, pointing off in the distance.

A short walk later, they were standing before Lisa's grave. Fresh flowers were all around it. It seemed so unusual that fresh flowers would be present since she had been dead for almost ten years.

"Does Mrs. Duet visit Lisa's grave daily?" he asked, not really expecting her to know the answer.

"Well, John, every time I visit your father, Lisa always has fresh flowers."

"Have you seen Mrs. Duet lately?" John questioned further.

"Not very much. She keeps mostly to herself since Lisa died. For several years after Lisa's death, she would come into the store and make a purchase now and then, but that was about it."

As they walked back to the car, John felt uneasy. He felt as though someone was watching him. It was hard to explain - call it a sixth sense - but while John had been in prison, he had fine-tuned this sense and was always aware of his surroundings. John looked over his shoulder, but could not detect anything out of the ordinary among the many headstones and monuments. Finally, John surmised that it must have been just a touch of paranoia.

John and his mother soon arrived home. The family's surroundings struck John in a way nothing had for some time. He was surprised to see his dad's old car in the drive.

"You kept the Mustang!" said John excitedly.

"You dad wanted you to have it when you graduated, so I kept it."

He was back home, in the place where he was raised. his room had remained unchanged for ten years. Though reminding him of happier days, the room no longer fit John's new personality. On the walls, banners of different football teams and several framed photographs of himself and Lisa were scattered throughout the room.

His mother had turned it into a shrine, never entering it; not even to clean, as the dusty furniture showed.

"Put your things down, and I'll start cleaning up in here. I didn't want to move a thing while you were in pri----"

Mrs. Braxton had said what she promised herself she wouldn't. She swore she would make no reference to the place that had kept her son for so many years.

Realizing his mother's uneasiness, John reassured her. "It's okay, Mom. Oh, by the way," John added matter-of-factly, "do you recognize this card?" He

VENGEANCE IS MINE

showed his mother the invitation he had received in prison.

"No, I haven't seen it before," she examined the card closer. "It must be someone's idea of a sick joke!" She said, visibly angered.

John walked over to his closet and opened the door. Inside, evenly spaced hangers held clothes long since out of style. It wasn't until that point that he realized he would need new clothes.

"Mom," John asked "do you think we could do some shopping tomorrow?"

"I'm already ahead of you," Mrs. Braxton said as she walked in with several shopping bags, "I went out yesterday and bought you enough clothes to get started with."

"We can't have our new store manager looking like he came through a time warp, now can we?" she asked, smiling.

"Go through some of your things, and what you no longer want we'll have the charity store pick up," Mrs. Braxton said as she walked to the door.

Stopping at the door, she turned to John. "It's good to have you home, son."

"It's good to be home," replied John as his mother closed the door behind her.

VENGEANCE IS MINE

VENGEANCE IS MINE

Chapter Thirteen

The next morning after breakfast, John and his mother left for the hardware store. The drive provided an opportunity to bring John up to speed about the changes the town had seen in the last ten years.

"John," Mrs. Braxton stated in a low, soft voice as though trying not to frighten him, "a lot has happened in ten years, and I want to know you're going to be all right. Fred, Paul, and Steve still live here in Houma. I hope what happened in the past is dead and buried." What she said brought back the memories of Lisa to both of them, but it was too late; she had already said it.

"Yes, she is," John said, referring to Lisa before she could say anything to avoid it. "Don't worry, Mom, I don't want trouble, I've had a lifetime's worth already. By the way, what are they doing now?"

His mother looked over to him, wondering if the only reason he asked was because it had come up in conversation. Maybe, she thought, he wasn't ready to let the past be, but after weighing the pros and cons, she decided to tell him. She knew he would find out sooner or later anyway.

"Fred works for the sheriff's department now. He's a deputy sheriff. Paul went into business for himself.

VENGEANCE IS MINE

He runs a small bar downtown. I hear tell he also takes bets on just about anything. Steve has turned into a full-fledged playboy, carefree and wealthy since he acquired his trust fund."

John did not say a word after she finished. He sat there emotionless as though in deep thought.

"And what happened to Judge Parker?"

Mrs. Braxton looked surprised by the question.

"I thought you knew, John. Hadn't I mentioned it on one of the trips to see you?"

"Mentioned what?" John questioned, his curiosity piqued.

"He's dead!" Mrs. Braxton exclaimed. "About a month after your trial, he was found shot to death in his house. The authorities believed he surprised a burglar and paid for it with his life. Ironic to think, about a month earlier he was passing sentence on your life when he himself only had a month to live."

"Yes," John replied, in a slow, deliberate voice as though he was still in deep thought. "Did they ever catch who did it?"

"No, they never did. They put a lot of time and money into it but came up without the killer. He covered his tracks pretty good. They were unable to find a single clue."

As they entered the business district, traffic began to thicken. Restaurants were already hard at work filling the air with pleasing aromas to beckon passersby.

Houma was an old town, founded in the 1800s and named for the Houmas Indiana, a small tribe of peaceful Indians who were the original inhabitants.

Old brick buildings, many of which had had recent facelifts to give them a more modern appearance, lined both sides of the narrow two-lane street.

VENGEANCE IS MINE

Mrs. Braxton turned into an alley which was just wide enough for one car. This led to a rear parking lot next to the bayou.

John and Mrs. Braxton entered the store from the rear of the building, as they had for as long as John could remember.

Just inside the steel door was a tall panel box where Mrs. Braxton was switching on the lights. Click, Click, Click. For each corresponding click, a light would awaken once more to illuminate the darkened building.

Leaving the storeroom when the light came on, John walked into the store.

Little had changed in ten years. The saws were still where they used to be, the nails still in their rotating bins where they had been for as long as he could remember. Within a few minutes, John had refreshed his memory of the store and couldn't help remembering his father as he had been. John remembered, as a small boy, running up and down the aisle and attempting to help any customer who would accord him the time. Memories of his dad were here more than any place else, probably because he spent more time here with his dad than any place else. As long as John could remember, his dad had worked sixty to seventy hours a week, leaving early in the morning and coming here late at night. Even on the weekend, his father found himself too exhausted to do little more than rest.

The morning went by relatively uneventfully with customers coming in and making small purchases and then leaving. John had recognized many of them from years back, but none of them either recognized him or wished to talk to him. But none of that bothered John because for the first time in years he felt happy.

VENGEANCE IS MINE

The bell rang, warning him of the approach of a customer. John looked up to see two police officers walk through the door. Both officers were dressed neatly in their highly polished shoes to their freshly pressed uniforms. Behind their mirrored sunglasses, John had not recognized either one until the first one removed the glasses and put them away in his pocket.

"Fred?" John gasped as he recognized his old nemesis. Losing his smile, his face slid into a stern frown.

VENGEANCE IS MINE

Chapter Fourteen

Mrs. Braxton spotted Fred about the same time John did. She put down what she was doing and quickly came to the counter, positioning herself between Fred and John.

"Listen, Fred, we don't want any trouble now."

"Trouble," Fred laughed. "There's no trouble. I heard John was in town and I wanted to come by and show him there's no hard feelings."

"May I speak with you for a second, John?" Fred asked in a most pleasant and disarming manner.

Seeing John's initial hesitation, he added, "Please."

Mrs. Braxton was caught totally off guard by Fred's sudden appearance, but her concern was obvious.

Fred seemed out of character to John, too polite. Could Fred have changed this much? John wondered, as he and Fred walked to the storeroom.

"How was prison?" Fred asked in a much harsher voice than when he was in earshot of Mrs. Braxton.

"I survived," John said, folding his arms across his chest and staring at Fred, who was pacing back and forth in front of him.

"I see you survived. I just hope you learned your lesson. Nobody screws with me and gets away with it."

VENGEANCE IS MINE

John remained silent, giving Fred all the time he needed to finish.

"I'm going to be watching you. You step out of line one time, and I'll bust you. Do I make myself clear?" Fred had stopped pacing at this point and had begun poking John in the chest.

John remained undaunted, staring Fred straight in the eye.

With that, Fred left, returning to the counter where Mrs. Braxton and his partner were waiting.

"Thank you so much, Mrs. Braxton. It was nice seeing you again. Have a nice day," Fred said, once again sporting a smile that concealed the real monster.

No sooner had Fred gone out the front door than Mrs. Braxton started bombarding her son with questions.

"What did he want?" Mrs. Braxton asked, curiosity all but consuming her.

"Fred just wanted me to know there were no hard feelings," John told his mother, not fully elaborating on the whole content of their conversation.

"Well," Mrs. Braxton said, relieved by the answer John gave her. "Maybe he's changed." She smiled, and returned to what she was doing.

John hated lying to his mother, but he felt it was far better to tell her a little lie than for her to worry herself into a frenzy. Besides, who would they believe - a fine, upstanding officer of the law, or a convict who was sent to prison for trying to kill Fred? It was clear in John's mind that he would have to give Fred a wide berth, not wanting to antagonize him. Too soon, that is.

Time passed quickly the first day, and soon John and his mother were heading home once more. On the way home, John realized that he would have to start all over again, making friends and getting out. It wasn't going to be easy, especially with Fred constantly looking over his shoulder.

John and his mother spent a pleasant evening together. After eating the magnificent pot roast his mother had prepared, John sat around and talked to his mother, more for her to catch up than for him. After a couple of hours, John rose to excuse himself.

"I think I'll take a little walk," John replied, reaching for his jacket.

"That's a great idea, Mrs. Braxton said. "I think I'll join you."

"No!" John exclaimed, startling Mrs. Braxton momentarily. Upon seeing her expression, John searched for an explanation for his response.

"Mother," John started in a soft tone, putting his mother a little more at ease. "There is nothing I would like more than to go for a walk with you. But try to understand, I'm going to need some time. Time alone to clear my head. Can you understand?"

"Sure, son, take all the time you need, but please be careful."

"Sure, Mom," John replied as he kissed her on the cheek, then closed the door behind him.

VENGEANCE IS MINE

VENGEANCE IS MINE

Chapter Fifteen

Through the darkness crept the silhouette. Slowly separating the blades of the sugarcane as it walked down the rows. Closer now, up ahead a red Mercedes at the end of the dirt road sat paralleling the field. A little closer and its occupants came into view. Within yards of the Mercedes now, the dark form observed for a while. Shrouded by cane, it remained undetected, watching, waiting, "remembering".

Steve Wakeman was good-looking and wealthy, every girl's dream. He was the stereotypical playboy; flashy cars, well dressed, and lots of money. Steve's only challenge in life was to see how quickly he could seduce the beautiful women he associated with. Once victorious, he would merely add another notch to his belt and move on to the next. A small town, however, had only so many beautiful women. It did not take long for Steve to go through the women in his age group. Thus starting the downward trend of dating younger women, until finally he was trying to conquer high school girls. This happened to be the case tonight. Picking up his naive counterpart at a discrete rendezvous point, Steve drove straight to the cane fields to avoid the risk of being detected. There in the cover of darkness, with the only witness the stars, Steve began his quest.

Steve and his young quarry held each other in a passionate embrace, kissing, bringing the fever of the moment higher and higher. The young girl had obviously thought this would be the limit to their passion. Though curious, there were still barriers she was not willing to cross at this early stage of her life. She felt she could trust the boys she had dates with, who in the past were always willing, though reluctantly, to stop when she demanded them to. This, however, was a totally different situation for her. Unlike the boys she had dated in the past, Steve was a man. A man used to getting his way. His heated passion would prove more than she could handle.

As their passion ignited the flames of desire to a fever pitch, Steve's hands began to explore the young girl's body.

Objecting immediately, she protested. "Stop!" she demanded in a firm, calm voice.

"Just relax," Steve responded, as he continued to explore the curves of her body with wandering hands.

"I mean it, STOP!" she said once again.

"No! I mean it, you little tease, you're not going to come this far and say no now!"

Fear shot through her as she suddenly realized the situation she had gotten herself into.

Steve reached over the other side of the bucket seat. Pulling a lever, that reclined the seat all the way back.

Then Steve climbed over to her seat, lying on top of her and continuing to kiss her, continuing to explore wherever he desired. Her muffled cries and pleas went unheard as Steve moved closer and closer to his goal, driven each step of the way by ego and desire.

VENGEANCE IS MINE

The dark form could see clearly into the car now from its vantage point. Steve lay on top of the girl as she struggled. The assailant moved from the cane now, gun drawn in its outstretched hand. It approached the car. Almost immediately upon leaving the cane, its movement was detected, but all they could do was look in horror at what they now saw.

Steve lay on top of her, moving closer and closer to yet another notch on his belt when he heard the rustle of cane nearby. Pausing only momentarily, he reasoned it to be an armadillo or other creature. When he finally realized what it was, it was too late. Lying on top of his date provided an excellent view from behind. There, not more than fifteen ears away, a figure walked towards him. The light cast from the partial moon gave a very clear picture of what was about to take place. A masked person held a pistol and had it pointing right at him.

"God, no!" Steve screamed as he lay helpless on top of his date.

To Steve's surprise the masked assailant did not shoot. Instead, he walked to the side of the car and opened the door.

"Get out!" he said in a raspy voice, motioning to the girl to leave.

Steve had already turned to the side allowing her easy exit, and she wasted no time running from the car, pulling her dress down as she went.

"Up to your old tricks, I see," the figure said as he reached into his pocket with his free hand.

"Who are you?" Steve asked. "Why are you doing this?"

The figure did not say anything, content in watching Steve squirm for a while.

VENGEANCE IS MINE

"Keys!" the raspy voice ordered.

Steve quickly removed the keys from the dash and handed them to the masked man.

Throwing the keys into the cane, the figure then displayed a pair of handcuffs.

"Steering wheel!" he demanded.

Steve, very eager to comply with the figure, made no attempt to provoke him, as the gun all the time was pointing to his head. Steve connected one ring of the handcuff to the steering wheel and the other to his own wrist, hoping this would appease the man from anything further.

"Is it money you want?" Steve asked, reaching for the dash and his billfold.

The figure opened the wallet and removed several bills that were inside, then threw the wallet back at Steve, striking him in the face.

The figure turned and disappeared into the cane stalks from which he had come.

Steve calmed down now, his heart slowing as his life was no longer held in the balance.

"Robbed," Steve thought, "all the way out here." He looked around for his date, but she was nowhere in sight. She had been so completely scared that she had kept running, never once looking back.

The sudden rustle of cane once again made Steve's heart pound. The figure parted the cane with one hand and held a can in the other.

Steve was puzzled. What else could this masked bandit want? He had taken his money and threw away his keys, yet he returned.

Fear cramped Steve's gut as he recognized the contents of the can... GASOLINE!

VENGEANCE IS MINE

"What are you going to do?" Steve inquired in a pleading tone as though he didn't already know.

The figure removed the top from the can and poured its contents into Steve's car and on to Steve.

"Stop!" Steve yelled. Yet his pleas fell on deaf ears, until finally the entire contents of the can were now on Steve and inside his car. The fumes burned his nostrils and eyes, as the vapors totally surrounded his area.

Steve yanked and pulled at the handcuffs violently. The steel of the handcuff began to cut into his wrist.

The figure calmly returned the cap to the gas can. Steve noticed how calm he was, how thorough he was, acting without emotion.

Reaching inside his overcoat, the figure displayed a large butcher knife. He paused for a moment to stare at the blade as though to weigh the knife's next assignment. After his moment of reflection, he tossed the knife on the seat of the car. Then he searched his pocket, finally pulling out a butane lighter and the money he had taken off of Steve a little earlier.

"You got one minute!" the figure said, looking at Steve.

Steve sat there in horror at the thought of what the figure wanted him to do. Either cut off his own hand to free himself or burn in the flames. Neither choice appealed to Steve.

As Steve grasped the butcher knife, he thought about taking a stab at this tormentor, but he wasn't close enough. If he threw it, the man would only sidestep it. Steve viewed his option as only one. Cut his wrist off and he might stand a chance of living, by playing out this sadistic individual's game. If not, he would surely die.

VENGEANCE IS MINE

Steve raised the knife high above his head, then paused, deciding to try to reason once more with this unknown sadist.

"Please!" Steve begged- "Don't kill me. You got my money. Just don't hurt me!" Steve paused momentarily as he started weeping. "What could I have possibly done to you to deserve this?" Steve asked, totally baffled as to the motives of his tormentor.

The figure slowly removed its mask, revealing to Steve for the first time its true identity.

"It's you!" Steve exclaimed. His eyes widened, and his face went pale from the discovery. Nothing could have prepared him for this moment because he had all but forgotten the reason why anyone would want to kill him. Only now in this brief second did he realize the depth from which this vendetta had come.

The figure looked at his watch, "Thirty seconds!" It shouted.

Frantically, Steve began whacking at his wrist with the butcher knife. Pain ached through his arm as blow after blow landed on his wrist. After only a couple of blows, the steel blade could be heard striking bone. CLANG! CLANG! The blade resounded as it chipped away at the bone. Swinging the knife at a fevered pace, Steve managed to cut through one of two bones in his wrist. Blood sprayed from his severed arteries, quickly turning the interior of the car to a crimson spray of blood, driven by his racing heart pumping his life's blood from his aching body. His arm had quickly turned into a pulverized mound of mangled meat dripping with blood. Steve screamed in agony as he experienced pain he had never known before.

Time, however, had run out as the figure lit the money and tossed it into Steve's car. The car was

VENGEANCE IS MINE

engulfed in a huge fireball. As the whole area lit up, Steve screamed and tried to break away but to no avail. Soon his screams stopped as his body was consumed with flames.

The figure retrieved the gas can and calmly disappeared into the cane field.

VENGEANCE IS MINE

Chapter Sixteen

The next morning, John and his mother went to work. The day started out normal as John went to his duties of inventorying the merchandise. All of a sudden, the front door slammed open.

"Where is he?" John heard someone yell to his mother.

John came from the back of the store to see Fred and his partner, with Fred in a verbal confrontation with his mother.

Upon seeing John approach, Fred grasped his holstered pistol.

"Put your hands on the counter!" Fred yelled as John continued to approach him.

John realized it was a very serious situation and complied, not wanting to give Fred any excuse to draw his pistol.

Fred held his position while his partner cuffed John.

"What the hell is this all about?" John asked as he straightened up and faced Fred.

Fred took his fist and buried it hard in John's stomach, knocking the wind out of him and doubling him over.

"You son of a bitch, you killed Steve!" Fred screamed, emotion having gotten the better of him.

VENGEANCE IS MINE

"Stop it!" Mrs. Braxton jumped in. "One more punch, one more mark and I'll slap the biggest lawsuit on you, it's going to make your head spin! What is my son being arrested for?" Mrs. Braxton demanded taking a position near her handcuffed son.

"For the murder of Steve Wakeman!" Fred responded.

"That's crazy!" said Mrs. Braxton. "John has been with me every minute since he got out of jail. He couldn't have killed Steve."

Mrs. Braxton's argument fell on deaf ears as Fred led John out to the patrol car.

"You remember what I said, Fred. Not a mark on him!" Mrs. Braxton said, as she returned to the store to close up and get her keys.

The drive to the courthouse did not take long. It was only four blocks away. Turning down into the underground parking garage, Fred pulled up directly in front of the elevators while John and Fred's partner got out and waited for Fred to park.

In the elevator, Fred started talking at John once again.

"You couldn't wait, could you? The first day you get out and you had to do Steve. Who was going to be next, Paul or me?'

John did not answer. He stood straight with his eyes forward. The elevator reached the top floor. Déjà vu came over him as he remembered ten years earlier when he had taken the same ride.

As the elevator door closed, John was pushed through the doors, only to come face to face with two Dobermans barking and growling. Their pearly white fangs snapped at John, trying to reach him. The only thing preventing them was a rather obese police officer

118

sitting in a chair directly behind the dogs. The officer held their leashes, preventing the savage beasts from tearing John to shreds. He just smiled as John regained his composure from the initial shock.

John was processed and then brought to booking where he would be photographed and fingerprinted.

Across the room, an important-looking man in his late thirties had just come out of the police captain's office. Fred wasted no time in rushing over to him and telling him of John's apprehension.

The man listened intently for a few moments, then unloaded on Fred. From his facial expressions, he was angry as he led Fred back into his office, this time slamming the door behind him.

After several minutes, the well-dressed man exited the office and walked up to John, who was still handcuffed.

"Mr. Braxton, my name is Jimmy Young. I'm the Assistant District Attorney for Terrebonne Parish," he said with an outstretched hand. Only then did he realize that John's hands were bound.

"Remove the cuffs," he ordered Fred's partner.

Fred's partner did not say a word but complied with Mr. Young's demand.

"I must apologize, Mr. Braxton, for the misunderstanding. The deputy was instructed to bring you in to answer some questions. I assumed he and his partner would have enough sense to grant you every courtesy," said Mr. Young, directing his statement more toward the deputy than to John.

"Well, mistakes happen," John said casually. "Apparently, you didn't know that Fred and I have a history."

VENGEANCE IS MINE

"I'm well aware of that fact now," said Young in a conciliatory tone.

Young turned to another officer who had just walked up.

"This is Detective Ben Clement," Young said, introducing the detective. "If you would be so kind as to answer a few questions for him."

"Would you mind coming with me to my office so we can talk," Detective Clement requested.

"Am I under arrest?" John asked, as he followed Mr. Clement to his office.

"No, John, but we would appreciate your cooperation. Sit down," Detective Clement said, motioning to a chair in front of his desk.

"As you may already know," Detective Clement said, "Steve Wakeman was killed last night."

"No, I didn't know," John said in a monotone, emotionless voice, "until Fred dragged me down here."

"How well did you know him?" Clement asked, sitting on the edge of his desk as he lit a cigarette.

"Not too well," John said, seeing where the conversation was leading, John decided to give Detective Clement a little of the background which had led to this point.

"Steve, your Gestapo deputy Fred, and one other person almost beat me to death ten years ago, but I haven't seen them since."

"Can you account for your whereabouts last night?" the detective pressed further.

"I don't know, Detective, do I have to account for my whereabouts?" John asked, starting to get angry at this point. The harness that had developed in him during his ten years in prison was beginning to surface.

VENGEANCE IS MINE

"Like I said earlier, we just want your cooperation," Clement said, trying to reassure and calm John.

"Sure," John said, "I was at home all night, with my mom."

The phone rang suddenly, interrupting the questioning momentarily.

"Hello, this is Detective Clement ... Yes, Sir! I understand, Sir. Yes, Sir, he has been reprimanded by the Captain."

John listened intently to the one-sided conversation. Hanging up the phone, Detective Clement turned to John.

"I am formally apologizing for the way you have been treated, I want to assure you the arresting deputy will be reprimanded. You are free to go."

John was surprised by the sudden turnaround. He suspected, but did not know at this point that his mother had something to do with it.

John took the elevator to the lobby where his mother was waiting.

"Did they hurt you?" she asked in a concerned tone.

"No," John assured her. "How were you able to get them to jump so high?" John asked, totally baffled by it all.

"Well," Mrs. Braxton started, "Mr. Morrison is the district attorney now. I don't know if you remember him or not. He was an old friend of your father's. Before you were released, I went to talk to him about any problems that might arise after you were released. I was mostly concerned about harassment from Fred. He was in a position where he had a little power, and I didn't want you to have any trouble. I never dreamed you would be questioned for murder. Well, when Fred left the store with you, I called Mr. Morrison and explained to him the way you were taken downtown and by whom. He made some phone calls, and here we are. Fred was abusing his authority, it's that simple. They have absolutely no evidence linking anyone, much less you, to Steve's death."

"John," his mother said in a soft voice, "I know it was only coincidence that you went out last night when Steve was killed, and I didn't mention it to the police. But I've got to ask, did you have anything to do with Steve's death?"

"Mother!" John responded in a hurt, almost wounded, tone. "How could you even think such a thing?"

"I'm sorry, son, I had to ask. There are a lot of people who would not blame you a bit for wanting vengeance, but it's not the way, John. You've got to put it behind you and move on."

"You're right, Mom. That's what I'm trying to do," John said, trying to reassure his mother and ease her already burdened mind. "Let's go to work," John said to her as they headed out of the station.

Back at the hardware store, John worked on a display of knives. He was trying to display the case in a manner in which the knives would jump out at customers as they passed. Trying various methods and liking none, John finally settled on a display in which the knives looked as though they were poised and ready to strike, blades up and the handles down. Exactly the opposite of what people were used to seeing.

For the next couple of days, John had a sense of uneasiness as though someone was watching him. As it turned out, his fears were not unfounded. While out on an evening walk, John spotted an unmarked sedan

VENGEANCE IS MINE

parked a couple of blocks away. The streetlight illuminated the rear of the car, casting just enough light inside to silhouette its occupants.

John stopped short, felt and patted his pockets, then his chest, as though he had forgotten something, and then returned to the house. Straight through the house and out the back door, John hopped over a neighbor's fence, through the yard to the next street, which ran parallel to his own. John was now one block over from the surveillance team. He went down two blocks, then up one; this put him right behind the sedan. John couldn't resist having a little fun with these guys. After all, it was going to be a long night for them. A little excitement might help break up the monotony.

John walked at a brisk pace. It was a beautiful night, nice and cool. Storm clouds had moved in, though, and it looked as though it might rain. John soon arrived in position behind the sedan. Crouching down, John was able to get right behind the car undetected. He could hear the murmurs of its occupants and the rustle of sandwich papers. This would be too perfect, John thought. Easing to the side of the car, he could see the windows were down.

John sprang up with a loud, "Hi, fellows!"

The sedan's occupants had been taken totally off guard. When John had sprung up, the two startled detectives were shaken so badly, the coffee they were holding sprayed on each other as their arm jerked with fright.

Realizing it was John, the detectives tried to wipe the coffee off the seat and themselves.

VENGEANCE IS MINE

John knew the two detectives would have loved to arrest him, but it would look pretty ridiculous if they arrested him for saying, "Hi."

John left them, laughing under his breath at how well his plan had worked. It was the first time in many years John had had fun and a reason to laugh. He had thought he had forgotten how. John wondered how long surveillance would be watching him. How long, he thought, until he could get back to a normal life...

VENGEANCE IS MINE

Chapter Seventeen

"Paul's Billiards and Bar" the red neon sign above the building read.

Paul had turned into quite an entrepreneur for a muscle-headed jerk. After high school, he had raised enough money (with the help of his parents) to open the bar and pool hall. This, however, was not the primary source of his income.

Paul ran a bookmaking operation in the rear of the building, which brought in the real money. Working until one or two o'clock in the morning was not unusual for him, and he worked mostly alone. This was the case tonight. Paul was alone.

The quiet streets of the early morning hour would summon no witnesses, no curious passersby. What was about to happen would remain unnoticed and unheard until morning.

Having parked the car a couple blocks away, the figure approached. Nearer to the building now, each step, each impulse, was driven by rage and vengeance. Paul's car was still parked outside the building, but was he alone? Moving down the side of the building, staying close to the wall and using shadows and darkness as its accomplices, the figure moved cautiously, methodically, to the rear of the building.

VENGEANCE IS MINE

The pool hall had been initially shrouded in a blanket of darkness, with the exception of one room in the rear. There, light pierced the darkness, giving a tip to the figure that its prey was still there. Maneuvering closer to the window, the figure crouched down just to the side of the opening.

Reaching into a pocket, the figure took only a few seconds to don a mask and gloves and prepare for what he had come for, what he had waited so long for. Tonight would be the night.

It would close yet another chapter in the figure's tormented soul. Paul, like Steve, would know tonight that the sins of the past do come back to haunt you.

He eased past the steel back door toward a window illuminated from inside. Its rays shone through the window and onto the ground, softly lighting the otherwise dark exterior.

Slowing rising to the edge of the window, he peered inside. The dirty window only partially obstructed his vision as he surveyed the interior of the room.

It appeared to have been an old storage shed that had been converted into an office. Several desks with phones on each were positioned in the center of the room, with heavy-looking binders stacked on each desk. On the walls around the room still remained tasteless decorations, remnants of the old storeroom. Old tools, some of which were antiques, old bridles, and several coils of rope all hung from the plank walls.

Paul sat at one of the desks, flipping through a binder and then writing something down on a pad. This went on for quite a while, until a crash of thunder startled both the watcher and the watched.

VENGEANCE IS MINE

Paul jumped as the flash of light and the crack of thunder shook him. Paul had been busy trying to close out his book tickets for the week. It had been an exceptionally good week with the high school games starting the season. Bookmaking always did better during the middle of the season and playoffs, although even then, there were ups and downs. What was so beautiful about this business was that there was always a season in one of several sports, and gamblers liked to bet on them all.

Deciding that the storm would surely bring a downpour, Paul decided to call it a night. Pulling his jacket off the back of his chair, he slipped it on while heading for the door. Turning off the lights, Paul unlocked the steel door and stepped outside.

Paul heard the electric charge click seconds before he fell to the ground in pain. He was paralyzed. He fought and struggled, but his body would not move. The stun gun had done its work effectively.

Paul broke out in a cold sweat when he saw his assailant standing over him, clothed in a black trench coat, gloves, and a mask. He stood over Paul, stun gun in hand.

He rolled Paul over on his side and grabbed his hands. Paul knew what the figure was doing when he heard the distinctive click of handcuffs being secured onto his wrists. The figure then dragged Paul back inside, closing the steel door behind him.

Several minutes, later, the effects of the stun gun had worn off, and Paul was able to once again move and talk.

"Who are you?" Paul demanded angrily, not taking into full account his situation.

VENGEANCE IS MINE

The attacker stood at the desk going through the books Paul had already examined.

"What do you want?" Paul demanded once more. "Money?"

The intruder remained silent, reaching into his pocket. The intruder displayed a pistol.

"Hey, hey," Paul said, not nearly as forceful as he had been earlier.

"We can make a deal," Paul bargained. "I've got money; you can have it. Besides, there's no reason to shoot me. I don't even know what you look like."

"Get up!" the masked intruder instructed, waving the gun at Paul.

Paul had difficulty at first, trying to stand, without the use of his hands, but soon he was on his feet, waiting for instructions.

Paul watched as the man removed a coil of rope that hung on the wall as part of the decor.

"Pool room!" he ordered, keeping the gun trained on Paul, ready for him to try something.

"Why are you doing this?" Paul asked, trying to understand what this person was after. If it wasn't money, he didn't know what it could possibly be.

"Get on the table!" the man ordered, motioning to the nearest table.

Paul was a good deal bigger than this unknown person and could have easily overpowered him, if he hadn't been handcuffed. Even then, a loaded pistol served as a great equalizer.

After Paul was positioned on the center of the table, his assailant shouted yet another demand. "Roll to your side," the man said in an increasingly agitated voice.

VENGEANCE IS MINE

Paul once again felt the voltage surge through his body. Paralyzed, his body lay motionless on the marble slab.

The assailant worked quickly, removing the cuffs and stretching Paul out across the pool table, then using the rope which he had taken off the wall, he secured Paul's arms with the rope, through the billiard pockets and then pulled it tight. He then secured it to his leg. He continued until each one of Paul's arms and legs were attached to a corner pocket.

Paul started coming out of his dazed state and heard the steel door slam. Paul felt relieved though puzzled that the man had left. The stun gun had left Paul dazed and a little disoriented as he pulled at his bindings.

Fear once again raced through Paul as the intruder reappeared in the doorway carrying a brown paper bag.

"What the hell do you want now?" Paul demanded.

Turning to Paul, the intruder pulled a large knife out of the paper bag.

"This is it!" Paul thought, his heart pounding hard, almost to the point he felt it would burst.

Instead of stabbing Paul with the knife, the attacker lashed away at his shirt, then pants, until finally Paul lay bound and totally exposed.

Paul's protests fell on deaf ears as his tormentor continued his work with speed and precision.

Returning the knife to the sheath, the masked assailant paused for a moment, making sure he had not left any loose ends.

Paul strained with all the strength he could muster, but the ropes were too strong. After a short while, Paul fell back to the table, his swollen and bleeding wrists all there was to show for his efforts.

VENGEANCE IS MINE

Paul looked over to the paper bag, where the intruder was carefully emptying its contents.

"Sterno!" Paul screamed, as several cans were removed from the bag.

Paul realized at this point what was finally going to happen, and he screamed at the top of his lungs.

"Help!" he yelled, but he knew no one would hear his cries.

The bar was located in a business part of town, thus eliminating the possibility of a neighbor hearing him. Traffic was almost non-existent this time of night, and even if a passing car did pass by, the sound would be so muffled it could not possibly be heard.

Paul yanked at his bonds once again, hoping to jerk free as his tormentor approached him with the Sterno.

Dipping his gloved hand into the can, he removed a large quantity and spread it onto Paul's chest. Paul fought till his exhausted body would protest no longer, finally being forced to submit to the Sterno application.

The Sterno felt cool as it spread across his body. Paul was one step ahead of his captor. He knew the flammable composition of the Sterno, and surmised what the next step would be. Several minutes and many more Sterno cans later, the intruder completed his task.

"Go ahead!" Paul demanded defiantly, realizing he was going to die no matter what he did. He wasn't going to give this man the satisfaction of begging for his life.

"What kind of animal are you?" Paul demanded. "Why don't you just put a bullet in my head and get it over with!"

The intruder once again paused to make sure he had not overlooked an empty can or cover, all the while

VENGEANCE IS MINE

constantly moving toward his final objective. The intruder gathered all the cans and returned them to the bag, along with the soiled gloves. No sooner had he removed the soiled gloves than he had put another pair on. Paul knew this person would never be caught. He was just too thorough.

Paul had all but conceded his fate, as he lay stretched on the pool table covered with Sterno. One thing he had to know before he died was why. Why was this person doing this to him?

The intruder turned toward Paul, holding the bag in one had, the other in his pocket.

"Just tell me why!" Paul screamed as he lay staring at his assailant.

The intruder did not say a word but reached for the mask, pulled it off, and placed it in the bag.

"My God!" Paul said, shocked by what he saw.

Just then, the intruder produced a lighter. Flicking it, he touched it to Paul's chest and started the slow spread of the blue flame.

Paul screamed as the heat grew more and more intense, spreading and burning him, sending agony throughout his body.

The intruder left, listening to Paul's screams, knowing the flames would not stop until all of the slow-burning Sterno was consumed.

A weight lifted from the intruder's chest as he could no longer hear Paul's screams. A sense of justice felt good to someone who had not known it. He disappeared once more into the shadows from which he had come, more like a ghost than a real human, not leaving a trace of his presence.

VENGEANCE IS MINE

Chapter Eighteen

As Detective Clement entered the poolroom, the smell of burnt flesh and smoke assailed him. Noticing the fingerprint man was finishing up, he went over to talk to him.

"Man, have you ever seen anything like this in your life?" the fingerprint man asked Detective Clement as he walked up.

"Not me. This is about the worst." Both men looked at what remained of Paul's body stretched out on the pool table. Small remnants of smoke still rose from the corpse, contributing still more to the already foul air.

The body still lay with its hands and legs stretched outward. Several small holes pierced the body, the fire burning through the flesh until all of the Sterno was consumed. It was a ghastly sight that would weaken even the strongest of stomachs.

The coroner had just finished gathering what information he needed, and, with the help of his assistant and a couple of police officers, they were able to load Paul's body, first from the pool table to a body bag and then onto a gurney.

"Got any ideas who might have done this?" asked one of the officers.

"None," responded Detective Clement, "And the killer is not making it any easier for us either. Once again, not a single clue! It's apparent that Paul had been making book for some time, maybe he was cutting into someone's territory and they decided to bump him off."

"Could be," the young officer replied, obviously not sold on the theory.

"Is there any chance that this murder and the Steve Wakeman murder are connected in any way?" The young rookie braced himself. It was not generally considered good practice to second-guess detectives.

Detective Clement paused for a moment as though in deep thought, then responded, merely saying, "It's too early to tell." He looked up at the rookie. "I want you to take a couple of men and sweep the parking lot and surrounding area. We're looking for a clue - any clue."

"I'll get right on it!" said the young rookie, eager to help in any way he could.

Detective Clement went to his car. Since the murder of Steve Wakeman, he had been the one responsible for placing the surveillance team to watch John Braxton's house. It was obvious that he did not have enough evidence to arrest John, and in any case, Fred had already tried that approach. His method would be different, more thought out. He would give John just enough rope to hang himself. Clement knew the killer was John; he felt it in his gut. All he needed was for the stakeout team to report him leaving the house and he would nail him. The rest of the puzzle would fall into place later, but at least he could get John off the street.

Clement picked up the receiver and called the officers who had John's house under surveillance.

VENGEANCE IS MINE

"Did he leave last night?" Detective Clement asked, anxiously awaiting the answer.

"No, sir, he didn't. His car has been in the driveway all night." The two officers were unwilling to divulge their little encounter with John. They knew it would make them appear incompetent.

"Very well," Detective Clement replied. "Keep the surveillance going until instructed otherwise."

Detective Clement sat in his car wondering, wondering how John could have somehow snuck out of his house and traveled halfway across town without being seen. Maybe he took a cab? The detective reasoned.

Detective Clement went to the nearest uniformed officer and told him what he wanted done.

"I need for you to check with all the cab companies in the area, see if they dropped a fare anywhere in this vicinity last night."

Detective Clement was grasping at straws. Two murders every six years were plenty for a small town like this. Now Detective Clement had two murders in a matter of days. The key suspect ironically enough had been supplied an alibi, courtesy of Detective Clement.

One thing was sure, a killer was loose in Houma, and he was powerless to stop him.

Fred heard about Paul's death from the police scanner. Catching only a few sketchy fragments, Fred had the blanks filled in by one of the men he worked with. Fred was worried now; he knew he would be next. But unlike Steve and Paul, he would be ready. He knew who the killer was. Even though there wasn't enough evidence, he knew. Besides, an arrest was not what Fred had in mind. He was going to take care of John in his own way, a final way.

VENGEANCE IS MINE

Fred got dressed and headed into town. It was about mid-morning now, and most of the shops had been open a while.

Pulling up in front of Braxton's hardware store, Fred parked his car and went inside. Before entering, however, he did spot the surveillance team watching intently.

Today was Fred's day off, and he wore western garb rather than his uniform, hoping he would attract less attention.

Walking up to the counter, Mrs. Braxton greeted him with caution.

"Can I help you?" she asked.

"Yes," he said in the most polite manner he was capable of. "I would like to speak to John if I may."

"Is there going to be trouble?" Mrs. Braxton asked, suspicious of Fred's motives.

"No, Ma'am, I just want to talk to him."

John had been busy stacking boxes in the warehouse and had not seen Fred come in.

"John!" his mother called, "Fred is here to TALK to you," giving emphasis to what she hoped Fred would do.

John came from the rear of the storeroom, dusting himself off as he walked.

"What is it now, Fred? You want to arrest me again?"

"No, just talk . . . in private?"

John looked at his mother, who had a concerned look on her face, clearly not really wanting to leave them alone.

With a nod from John, she reluctantly agreed.

"I'll be in the storeroom if I'm needed," Mrs. Braxton said, closing the curtain behind her.

"What can I do for you, Fred?" John asked.

VENGEANCE IS MINE

"No! I think it's what you can do for yourself! I know you killed Steve and Paul," Fred said in a much firmer voice than he had used earlier.

"Paul's dead?" John asked in surprise.

"Don't act surprised for my benefit," Fred said. "We both know what's going on here." "It's over, John! It stops right now."

"I don't know what you're talking about," John responded, showing little expression and no fear.

"Very well then, but I tell you this, if I see you anywhere around me, I'll put a bullet in you first, then ask why later. I'm not going to be number three on your list. I've got to hand it to you, though, you're smart, very smart, but when are you going to smarten up and realize what's done is done? What happened ten years ago is history!" Fred said in an embittered, angry tone.

"Sure, it's over for YOU! YOU didn't almost get beaten to death while the woman you loved was raped! YOU didn't spend ten years behind bars! YOU didn't bury the woman you loved! So don't talk to me about it being over! I'll carry what you three bastards did to me for the rest of my life!"

"Which will be a short one if you come at me! I'd watch my back if I were you! I think we understand each other," Fred concluded, barely able to contain his anger. Fred put his sunglasses on as he turned and left the store, not looking back.

John's mother came out from the storeroom. "What was that all about?"

"Nothing," John said, lying to his mother once more, "He just wanted to apologize for the other day."

"Really?" Mrs. Braxton said, not believing a word of it.

VENGEANCE IS MINE

Fred started his car and headed back home. He was going to have to be on his guard now. Unlike Steve and Paul, Fred knew he would be next.

But he would be waiting.

VENGEANCE IS MINE

Chapter Nineteen

Burt Young, reporter for The Courtier, had always taken pride in his ability to find a story where others had had failed. Today was to be no exception.

Burt had watched with increasing interest the last two brutal murders in his small town, which until recently had been unheard of.

While at the crime scene of Paul's murder, Burt had detected a small silver barrette along the way. It was very unique in its design. Burt knew he had seen it before - but for the life of him he was unable to place it. Choosing not to dwell on it for more pressing matters were at hand, Burt safely tucked the barrette away in his pocket.

The assailant watched as Burt put the barrette into his pocket. Not daring to venture nearer for fear of being recognized, the assailant remained a safe distance away, thinking, planning, biding his time.

He had felt fear for the first time when Burt found the barrette. Not because he feared being caught, for he viewed that as inevitable. The one thought which he feared most was not being able to finish what he had started.

It was unfortunate about Burt, he thought as he contemplated Burt's fate in his mind. Burt was an

VENGEANCE IS MINE

innocent outsider who was in no way connected to this. But because of his curious nature, he posed a definite threat to what he had to do. For if one thing was certain; he would not be denied vengeance, not after all this time.

Withholding evidence was not beyond Burt's scruples, by no stretch of the imagination. Nor were a few other things. "Whatever it takes to get the story," was Burt's motto.

Burt was a familiar face around the police station, always on a quest. The only problem was not too many big stories happened in a small town.

For as long as he could remember, the only thing he ever wanted to do was write. After graduating from Nicholls State University in Thibodaux, there was little doubt what he would do; investigative reporting. Along with such a profession had to come the commitment, which no one could argue Burt had, but sacrifice was the next ingredient which determined if an individual caught his dream, not just chased it. Burt had lived nowhere else. His family and friends were all in Houma. He would often rationalize the many reasons that kept him in Houma. Most of the time, it was when he was evaluating his career. he knew if he was ever to be the reporter he desired, he would have to leave, but for now he settled for being a dead head reporter in a dead head job.

"Hiya, Jimmy!" Burt called as he walked up to the young rookie, apparently posted there to guard the area.

"Oh hi, Mr. Young," Jimmy replied, cordial though obviously not overjoyed to see him.

"What have we got here, Jimmy?"

VENGEANCE IS MINE

Jimmy looked at Burt, parted his lips as though to speak, then paused. "I'm not at liberty to comment on an ongoing investigation," he finally replied, in a fashion which led Burt to believe the statement had been rehearsed many times before.

"Cut the bullshit, Jimmy. The public has a right to know! Off the record, what's going on?"

"OFF THE RECORD!" Jimmy blurted out, momentarily losing his composure. "The last time I talked off the record to you, I had my ass in a crack for a month!"

Though he never named his source, Jimmy was one of the few people to have access to the specific information outlined in the article, which made him the prime suspect as a source. His superiors knew it was him, and they had made it clear through subtle little comments. It was nothing blatant, just enough to let him know they knew. Thank goodness no one really cared for the mayor anyway, or the scenario might have been quite different. He reasoned now, however, that his superiors felt he had learned his lesson. They were right; Jimmy swore he would never again put himself in a situation like that again.

"Come on, Jimmy," Burt tried to reason, "Let's let bygones be bygones."

Burt realized this was one bridge he had burned and was unrepairable. Too bad, he thought, he kind of like the kid.

No sooner had Burt finished talking to Jimmy than Detective Clement came through the door.

"Is he giving you a hard time?" the detective asked, addressing his question to the rookie.

"No, sir, I was just explaining to the gentlemen that this is a crime scene and the area is restricted."

VENGEANCE IS MINE

"Very good, Officer," Clement replied. "He apparently has difficulty understanding. Let me try to explain it to him, may I borrow this?" the detective asked, not waiting for an answer as he lifted the nightstick from the ring on the officer's belt. "Sir, would you come with me now?" The detective ordered as he indicated a direction to the front of the building.

The police force had changed dramatically over the past ten years, and slowly, one by one the bad police officers had been weeded out.

Although reduced, police brutality still existed. It was a part of the mentality of the older officers who got a rush from the power of the office.

Detective Clement, although not a bad cop by most standards, was not beyond using force on whoever and whenever he felt a point had to be made. This was his reputation, and no one pushed the issue enough to provoke him.

The rookie watched as they turned the corner, "He's going to get it now," he thought. Clement just didn't want any witnesses."

Burt walked to the front of the building with Clement close behind.

"That's far enough!" Clement said as he touched the nightstick to Burt's shoulder.

Burt turned around to see Clements's outstretched hand. "How the hell are you, Burt?" Clement said, shaking the hand of his old friend.

"Still messing with rookies, I see," Burt grinned.

"Yes, Burt, they still think I'm the baldest kid on the block, and the older you get, the more you have to rely on perception rather than fact."

"What you got here?" Burt asked, falling back into his reporter mentality.

VENGEANCE IS MINE

"It's Paul Guidry. He was tortured and set on fire."

"Like Wakeman?" Burt asked, recalling the similarity.

"Yes, but instead of gasoline, they used Sterno. I guess they wanted him to last a little longer."

"Any leads so far?" Burt inquired, knowing the dead end the police department had reached in the Wakeman investigation.

"None, not s single clue. We only have one suspect, but we've had him under surveillance since Steve's death."

"What's the suspect's name?"

"It's John---Oh no! You're not going to get that out of me. First thing you know, you'll be running an article quoting me!"

"Now, Ben, I sense you don't trust me."

"Damn right I don't. I know you. I got to finish up," Clement indicated as he once again shook Burt's hand. "Now get out of here before you get arrested."

Burt left the scene and headed for the newsroom, all the while trying to place the barrette. It was almost noon when he reached the newspaper. The sun shone brightly in the cloudless sky. Normally, Burt would have taken at least a couple of minutes to enjoy the day. Today, however, his thoughts were elsewhere.

VENGEANCE IS MINE

VENGEANCE IS MINE

Chapter Twenty

"Where have I seen it?" he thought, trying to fish the thought up from his memory.

Burt pulled up to the rear of the newspaper where he always parked and entered through the double doors of the rear entrance.

Upon entering the office, he heard the resounding voice of an individual that he had tried to avoid.

"Where's the story on the Mayor's news conference?" the editor demanded, apparently already knowing the answer.

"I was unable to make the conference," Burt replied. " I had to ---"

"I know you had to go to the crime scene;" the editor interrupted. "Burt, let me tell you something. I assign the stories here. You either follow my instructions or you can find yourself another newspaper. Do I make myself clear?"

"Crystal!" Burt replied, realizing it was the only way to defuse the situation. It was not a good time to reason with him.

Things had changed drastically for Burt within the last six months. Burt's previous boss had always had a much looser style of management, leaving Burt to pursue stories he felt strongly about. The old editor

VENGEANCE IS MINE

didn't really care, just so the story was good and on time.

This dramatically changed after his retirement. Replaced with a manager from a large newspaper, who took an immediate dislike to Burt from the start. He had made Burt's life miserable, assigning him to stories which were of little substance and keeping him under close watch. This, like many other obstacles Burt had had to overcome, would also be overcome. Only this time, Burt had no idea how.

Burt headed for the microfilm room, hoping to find a clue to the silver barrette. Reel after reel Burt searched, losing all sense of time. Finally, just when he was ready to end the exhaustive search for the clue to the barrette, the answer hit him

Burt stared at the screen in disbelief. In that brief second, it all fell together. Though the motive for Steve and Paul's death was clear now, Burt had more difficulty believing who the killer was.

Burt pressed a button which activated a printer. After a moment while the printer spat out a hard copy of the microfilm, Burt lifted the sheet up and stared into the eyes of the murderer, the eyes of ---

"What was that?" Burt thought, startled by the loud slamming of a heavy door.

Burt quickly folded the photo, wrapping the barrette inside. Turning the screen off, he tucked the photo and barrette between the monitor and the computer.

Burt cautiously peered out into the hall. It was only then did he realize how late and how alone he was.

The thought of having identified the killer and being all alone in the massive building played havoc with his imagination. Every little sound Burt misconstrued as sinister in origin. Burt could hear his breathing as his

VENGEANCE IS MINE

pulse raced. His heart pounded like a kettledrum, the sound gradually growing louder and faster. Perspiration began to bead on his forehead as he loosened his tire.

Maybe it was the boss leaving, he reasoned, walking to the window looking out on the parking lot. The chill returned as Burt realized his boss's car was gone.

Puzzled, Burt began to think to himself. "Who would possibly still be here this late at night?" Burt looked up at the clock on the wall to see it was 1:15 A.M. Burt looked around. Not seeing anyone, he called out, "Hello, is anyone there?"

Silence followed. Burt felt an uneasiness swelling inside of him, something between fear and panic.

"Hello," Burt called out once more. "Is anybody here?" he called, his words echoing in the large building.

Then footsteps! A door somewhere opened and shut, removing any doubt that he was alone. Burt moved forward to investigate. Slowly and cautiously, Burt moved around the desks that made up the newsroom. Moving into the hall, he peered at the darkened hall that led to the mailroom.

Burt opened the door leading into the darkened mailroom and walked across the threshold. Searching for a switch to light up the high, dark room, his hands slapped against the cold wall. After a short search, Burt found it, then switched it on.

Nothing Happened!

Burt flipped the switch on and off again several times, each time hoping it would be the one to illuminate the darkness, but to no avail. Footsteps echoed off the concrete walls. Burt strained into the darkness, trying to determine who was there.

VENGEANCE IS MINE

"Okay, guys, this isn't funny anymore," Burt called out, thinking someone was playing a practical joke on him.

Burt had, in the past, been guilty of pulling pranks on his fellow employees, and he knew one day he would get paid back. Maybe today was the day.

Burt was feeling very uneasy. He waited for one of his coworkers to jump out and scare him. They would have a good laugh, and it would be over. But it never happened. As Burt walked around the still machinery, he looked and listened. He could neither see nor hear anything. The footsteps he had heard earlier had faded and had not been heard again.

Suddenly, Burt heard the sound of the huge three-story printing press as it was switched on by some unknown person. The mailroom was next to the pressroom, and the vibrations from the big machine drummed through the room. The loud noise of the press concealed any movement which might have been heard. Burt crossed over into the pressroom. The area around the press was dimly lit by emergency lights. There was just enough light to clearly make out a note that had been attached to the press. Burt removed the note from the press and angled it so the most light would be cast on it.

He read:

"You should have minded your own business!"

Panic-stricken, Burt realized this was not a joke!

Burt never heard a thing, just a sudden pain in his back and chest, bringing him to his knees as all strength left his body.

Burt looked down to discover a bloody shaft protruding out of his chest. It was a broom handle broken to form a ragged point. It was the last image

VENGEANCE IS MINE

Burt saw, as his blurry eyes rolled back and he toppled over dead.

Searching through Burt's pockets, the assailant could not find the barrette! The reporter could have put it anywhere, he thought. Reasoning that he did not have time to conduct a search, he left the building the way he had entered. Besides, he thought, by the time they put it all together, it would be over anyway. Justice would have been served and vengeance satisfied.

VENGEANCE IS MINE

VENGEANCE IS MINE

Chapter Twenty-one

Fred hastily threw clothes into his suitcase. Having asked for time off, Fred was planning to take a week and go up to the family cabin outside of town. Fred realized, as did others, that the recent deaths of two of his close friends had made him a bundle of nerves, and extremely paranoid. Fred had no doubt in his mind that John would be coming after him next, and Fred would be ready. Going to the cabin would allow him time to think, to plan. Also, it would provide a safe haven. He would be able to detect anyone coming before they got too close. Fred closed the suitcase, putting a knee on top to force it down.

Locking the house, Fred headed for his car, his paranoia still in tow. Carefully, he examined the surrounding area, even though he didn't know exactly what he was looking for. How would John come after me, he wondered, recalling the tortured deaths of his two friends. How could Paul have been taken off guard? He couldn't help feeling he had not done enough for his friends. One thing was sure, though; he would avenge them.

The problem that lay before Fred was how to kill John without everybody suspecting him, as they surely would. He needed a plan with an airtight alibi.

VENGEANCE IS MINE

Fred opened the trunk and put his suitcase inside. Closing the lid, Fred once again scanned the area.

"For Rent," the sign read, indicating the deserted nature of the old buildings. The high unkempt shrubs proved ideal for surveillance.

Crouched behind the bushes, the assailant watched as Fred walked to his car, suitcase in hand. "What!" he thought for a moment, his plans for Fred's demise temporarily thwarted. He had planned to douse Fred's house with gas and then ignite it, creating an inferno that Fred would probably not survive. But if he did, a silent arrow delivered by a crossbow would ultimately end his miserable life.

But now Fred was leaving. Maybe this would work out better, he thought. He would follow Fred. The deputy's false sense of security might cause some carelessness...

Fred quickly made his way out of town. Within minutes, he was on Highway 90, which would take him to the cabin. The ride gave him lots of time to think, think about what brought him to this point. He could still see the mental pictures in his mind of that night. He could still hear Lisa's pleas, yet he still felt no remorse about raping Lisa, which had eventually driven her to suicide. What he regretted now more than anything else was the fact that he had not finished John off when he had had the chance.

Fred thought about how it would have been ten years ago when his dad was in charge. Someone like John would simply turn up missing, saving the taxpayers the expense of a trial.

The old days, Fred reflected. He had hired onto the police force right after high school and his acquittal. This was when the changes had started. It had been en election year, and Lisa's death and John's incarceration were still fresh in everyone's mind. Fred's father was soundly defeated. Even after spreading an enormous amount of money around, he still had been defeated.

The new Sheriff had run on a platform of change, and had wasted no time in showing the change he was after. Quickly, officers practicing old police Gestapo tactics were fired and replaced with new officers who were sincere, as far as the Sheriff could tell, in their efforts to protect and serve.

Although the Sheriff had targeted Fred many times, he was unable to get anything on Fred. The sheriff looked upon Fred as a symbol of the past, and he would continue to try to eliminate him, whatever it took.

As Fred rounded a curve, a large road sign came into view.

"SCHRIEVER"

Time seemed to have just flown by. Before Fred realized it, he was at the end of his journey.

Fred loved coming up to the cabin. Located on a small manmade lake, it often served as a retreat for him, and offered an opportunity to get away. With no phones and no neighbors, the cabin provided quiet solitude, just what he needed about now.

Turning off the main highway, Fred took a private dirt road that led to his cabin. The car kicked up a cloud of dust behind it as it sped down the narrow road. The private road, only about a mile long, was just wide enough for one car to travel at a time. Trees lined both side so close to the road that if two cars met on the road, one would have to back up.

Soon, the road opened into a large clearing, and there nestled among the oaks overlooking the lake was the cabin.

VENGEANCE IS MINE

It was only a two-bedroom structure with a kitchen and a large family room. Made from logs, the cabin seemed like something Davy Crockett would have lived in. But Davy Crockett had never known the convenience of electricity, dishwashers, microwaves, and other appliances that occupied this modern dwelling.

Fred parked his car right outside the cabin and retrieved his suitcase from the trunk.

Opening the front door, Fred's first view of the interior was one of scattered sheets covering various furnishings, giving the impression of ghostly figures waiting to pounce.

Placing his suitcase in the corner, Fred quickly moved to arrange the inside of the cabin into quiet comfort.

After about an hour of cleaning and straightening up, Fred was satisfied enough with the cabin.

Fred made a thorough check of the house's windows and locks. Having done so, he started a fire in the fireplace. The dry kindling and well-seasoned wood soon brought forth a nice fire. Returning with a double bourbon he had found in the cupboard, Fred settled back on the couch and stared at the fire, thinking. Thinking about the deaths of his two friends. Thinking about how he needed to kill John.

With the reassuring warmth of the fire and the sense of security the cabin brought, it wasn't long before Fred was drifting off to sleep.

Sleep had been something Fred had not been able to get a lot of lately, ever on guard for John to try to kill him for what had happened ten years ago.

Fred slept and dreamt, and in all of his dreams and recollections, Fred's mind brought forth memories from

VENGEANCE IS MINE

years past, ten years to be exact, to a night where he and his friends had destroyed two lives.

Fred looked at the images his mind had recalled. It was not as he had seen them some ten years ago. Instead of reliving the memory through his own eyes; it was as though he was witnessing the scene from an elevated position. He could see himself as though he was viewing a previously recorded movie. Everything seemed so clear, so real, unlike hazy dreams of the past.

VENGEANCE IS MINE

Chapter Twenty-two

Detective Clement was more baffled now than before. Murders were taking place randomly, he thought as he headed toward The Courtier, having received the call on Burt's death. Detective Clement immediately radioed the surveillance team assigned to John.

"No, Sir, he didn't move all night," was the unwelcome response.

This was disheartening news for the detective, who was already receiving a lot of heat from the mayor's office to solve this crime wave, and do it quickly. One more death would only exacerbate the situation. With no clues, and the only suspect under twenty-four-hour surveillance, Detective Clement was at a loss on just how to solve this case. He only hoped something, anything, would break and give him a clue ... a direction.

"Of all the times for this to happen," Clement thought. Clement had found himself in the middle of a bitter divorce and custody battle, which had taxed his emotions to breaking point.

His wife of twenty years had simply come home one day and asked for a divorce. Tired of his irregular hours, she sought a more structured lifestyle. Hell,

VENGEANCE IS MINE

Clement didn't blame her. In fact, he was surprised it had lasted as long as it did. Over recent years, he was seldom hone, and when he was, he devoted all his time to his son. In retrospect, he realized he should have taken care of her emotional needs, but that was now history.

The divorce had started off fine until she made her plans known to take their small son of six and move up to Shreveport with her parents. Clement couldn't bear the thought of only seeing his son on holidays, which in essence would be the only time he could get off. Committing himself to the goal of obtaining custody, Clement embarked upon the expensive road of lawyers, courtrooms, and hearings, never really knowing how it would ultimately end.

Now, along with everything else going on in his life, a psychotic killer was on the loose, threatening to rob him of the only thing his wife had not taken away: his job. Clement knew if he didn't solve this case and solve it quickly, he would be replaced. This sobering thought drove Clement constantly, affecting his sleep and eating habits. Then when he thought nothing else could possibly happen to him, it did. Not only was there another murder, it turned out to be a friend he had seen only hours earlier.

Clement recollected back to when he and Burt had met hours earlier. Did Burt discover something about the murders? Or was this some sick signal to him, a flagrant taunt which confirmed his utter helplessness in solving the case?

It was early in the morning when Detective Clement arrived at the newspaper. The sun had only just risen, yet a small crowd of curious onlookers had already gathered.

VENGEANCE IS MINE

Being kept back by uniform police, the bathrobe-clad crowd seemed to have just gotten out of bed. Comprised mostly of surrounding residents, they were waiting to get a glimpse or at least an idea of what was happening inside the building. Up until now, curiosity had kept them glued to the spots, not allowing them to leave.

Clement pushed his way through the crowd and came face to face with one of the uniformed officers.

"Detective Clement," he said, showing the officer his identification and badge, then continued toward the building.

Entering the pressroom, he noticed all the activity was in the far corner. Zigzagging his way around equipment and man high rolls of paper, he finally reached the site.

"What we got here?" Detective Clement asked, walking up to the officer in charge.

"A pretty messy killing," was the response from the middle-aged lieutenant. "Burt Young, run though with part of a broom handle!"

"Any clues picked up so far?" Clement asked, feeling overdue for a break.

"No, not yet, just the broom handle. We already dusted it for prints, but it was clean."

"What do you make of all these killings?" Detective Clement asked the officer.

"I'm just as puzzled as you are. At first, I thought it was someone out to settle a score. But now Burt, he never hurt anyone."

"Unless?" Clement joined in.

"Unless what?"

"Unless he was working on something which would had led us to the killer."

VENGEANCE IS MINE

"That's a possibility."

"Check with his supervisor and find out all you can on what he was working on. Also, go through his desk and the entire buildings inside and out, even the trash."

"What are we looking for?" the officer asked, realizing the magnitude of the assignment.

"Anything!" Clement replied. "We're well overdue for a break."

Just a few short weeks ago, everything was fine. His career had been going well, and there was even some talk about him running for Sheriff. Now, in light of the recent killings, not only was his future political aspiration shelved, he had to watch his back. He was beginning to realize that if he did not solve these killings, he would without a doubt be used as a scapegoat. This thought scared him more than anything, for he knew men of power could destroy anyone if they deemed it necessary. He had worked too hard to get this far; he would not be used.

VENGEANCE IS MINE

Chapter Twenty-three

The assailant watched from the trees. He had tailed Fred to this deserted location and could not have asked for a better situation; Fred alone and isolated. He would have time with Fred. Time was something he had not had much of with the other two, but now he would have the time to make Fred suffer, make him beg like Lisa had. He vowed Fred would search for mercy but find none. Fred would pray for death, yet it would elude him. He would only die when he had suffered enough.

Darkness had fallen now, and the only light visible from his vantage point was that of the moonlight shining softly on the lake, and that of the intermittent shadows and firelight in the window of the cabin.

He crept closer to the cabin now, confident in the belief that Fred was sound asleep.

It was about midnight now as he walked toward the cabin. Having crouched down in the bushes for over four hours, it felt good for him to stretch.

Crossing the small clearing, he placed his back against the log wall next to the living room window. Peering around the edge, he could see clearly into the cabin. The only light in the room was that from the fire. There was Fred lying on the couch with a whiskey glass still in his hand. He moved toward Fred's car and knelt beside a tire. Removing a knife from its sheath, he inserted it slowly into the side of the tire. Air rushed out and caused a high-pitched squeal as it eventually deflated. He did the same to the three remaining tires. Before leaving the area, he spotted an ax which was stuck in a tree stump used to cut firewood. 'I could use this,' he thought, wiggling the handle to free the blade.

Traveling back down the narrow lane with the ax by his side, he scanned each side of the road. About a quarter of the way down the road, he found what he had been looking for; a pine tree large enough to block the path of a vehicle.

Crack! The ax swung downward, removing a large chip of wood from the tree. The silent forest only magnified the sounds of the tree as its v-shaped gouge grew larger and larger. Finally, slowly at first, the tree started to lean toward the road. A few more quick chops on the back side sent the tree crashing down.

The tree lay across the road with no way around it. The rat was trapped!

He then returned to his vantage point to wait, to watch. He wanted Fred to know, to remember, to be afraid. Then when Fred had tasted fear, he would taste death slowly, very slowly.

Fred awoke to the smoldering remnants of a fire, which only a few hours earlier was ablaze.

Picking up his suitcase from the corner where he had put it earlier, he tossed the overstuffed luggage on the bed. Pressing the two clasps, he removed his shaving kit. Fred headed for the bathroom for a quick shower and shave.

Fred casually proceeded with the activities of the morning. He felt good, and most of all he felt safe. There was something about the old cabin that made

VENGEANCE IS MINE

Fred feel good. Lord knew he hadn't felt good in a while. Only now did he realize the stress he must have been under, as now a sense of serenity filled him as he continued around the cabin.

After showering, Fred dressed in casual clothes. He had planned on possibly taking a walk in the woods or along the lake. It was going to be a beautiful morning. He could hear the ducks on the lake, as one duck began to quack, then others joined in. High in the pine trees, Fred also heard the squirrels barking to one another.

Heading out, Fred stopped only for a soft drink out of the refrigerator. They had been in there for quite some time, but the empty refrigerator had little else to offer. Fred pulled the soft drink out, immediately popping the top on the way to the porch. A balanced breakfast was something Fred had not known in many years. The extent of breakfast for Fred was a pot of coffee if he had time to make it, or had remembered to set the timer the night before. If not, Fred would have a Coke for breakfast.

Walking out to the small porch of the cabin, Fred looked out over the lake. He recalled how his father had chosen this particular place. It was miles around the lake to the next nearest camp, and the only way in or out was on a private road.

Fred took a sip of his Coke and casually looked around. He stopped suddenly when his car came into view. Two of his tires looked flat.

Leaving the porch, he walked over to his car and knelt beside one of the tires.

Fred dropped his Coke can and looked around, expecting at any moment to be attacked. Fred knew he was in danger when he saw the large gash in the side of the tire. Quickly, Fred turned and ran back inside the

163

VENGEANCE IS MINE

cabin to his suitcase where he pulled his revolver from its holster. Returning to the living room, he peered through the curtains.

This son of a bitch is playing games! Fred thought as he kept a vigilant lookout trying to detect any movement.

Fred began realizing the situation he had put himself in. He was safe as long as he stayed in the cabin, but as soon as he left, he became a sitting duck. John, he thought, could pick him off at any time. No phone, very little food, and in Fred's haste, he had failed to notify anyone of his whereabouts.

The only solace Fred had was the fact that he did have a pistol but no extra shells. Six shots would be the only chance he had.

Still by the window, Fred settled down for the long wait. Sitting next to the window, he was just tall enough to peer out over the sill. He watched and waited.

After a long time, Fred came up with a plan. Fred knew his best chance would be at night. He would drive the car to the main highway, riding the rims if necessary. If nothing else, he could possibly receive help from a passing motorist.

Time passed slower than Fed had ever known before. While waiting, Fred's mind drifted to other things: Steve and Paul. No way was he going to suffer their fate, he thought, and if the worst should happen, he was determined to take John with him.

Darkness had fallen, and the time just after sunset and before the moon rose would be the darkest hour, thus giving Fred the best possible chance of escaping. If he could get started, he knew his chances would be

VENGEANCE IS MINE

good because it would be extremely hard to hit a moving target.

Fred took one last long look out the window, with his keys in one hand and his pistol in the other, he was prepared to make a run for it.

Flinging the cabin door open, Fred darted out, not caring about the open door he was leaving. At this point, he could care less if the whole cabin burned down. All Fred knew was he had to get away, get help. He couldn't wait John out, he knew. He would eventually have to come out sooner or later. Why not now when he still had the strength to make a run for it?

Fred jumped off the porch, and in two steps, he reached his car. Using his left hand to unlock the door, Fred held his pistol in his right and scanned the tree line. It was far too dark for Fred to see beyond the trees, and he knew at this point he was the most vulnerable. If he did see a muzzle flash, maybe he could return fire. With a little luck, he might take out his assailant.

Seconds seemed like hours, until finally the lock turned; the door was pulled open, and Fred was inside. Laying the pistol on the seat next to him, he quickly started the engine. Fred slammed the car in reverse, then into low gear, turning the car toward the road set between the trees.

Fred could not make out the road. It was too dark. he could have turned his light on, but that would have only presented a much easier target. Speeding down the road, he navigated his way out to supposed safety.

The assailant watched as Fred hastily attempted his escape. He didn't run. He calmly walked down the road toward the fallen tree, crossbow by his side.

VENGEANCE IS MINE

The night had started to lighten as he walked. The freshly kicked up dust remained suspended still as he moved.

He heard the crash: metal being twisted, glass shattering, and branches snapping beneath the force of the impact.

He walked on, never increasing his pace. After all, he thought, this is a time to be savored, not rushed.

VENGEANCE IS MINE

Chapter
Twenty-four

Fred never saw the tree, he had smashed into it head on, sending his body slamming into the steering wheel and windshield. Something was warm in his eye, Fred thought as he began to regain consciousness. Each move he made only magnified the immense pain his body was in. He knew his forehead was cut, and he knew he had some cracked ribs. If there was anything else damaged, the pain from his head and ribs drowned it out for now.

Fred sat back in his seat, regaining awareness of his surroundings little by little. As he leaned back, however, through the rearview mirror he saw a figure walking towards him. Fred's adrenaline started pumping. Momentarily forgetting his pain, he searched in the darkness for his pistol, it was no longer on the seat. Immediately searching the floorboards, he groped for the pistol which had apparently been thrown off the seat during the crash. Search as he might, he was unable to come up with the pistol.

Straightening back up, he glanced in the rearview mirror once more. The road had become somewhat illuminated by the moonlight. There walking down the road was a sinister figure. Fred knew he had to move fast. Opening the door, Fred tried to exit but was

VENGEANCE IS MINE

overwhelmed by pain from his ribs. He fell to the ground beside the car on his hands and knees. Fred knew the figure wasn't far away. His only hope was to run into the woods and hide. Mustering every bit of his strength, he got to his feet and darted into the woods. Before he had gotten ten yards, Fred had fallen twice. Each time, the pain from his injuries zapped a little more of his strength. Falling the third time, Fred lay motionless on the ground and listened. He heard his car door slam, followed by silence. Fred waited and listened to see if the assailant would enter the woods. Fred knew he would be able to hear him coming, but could Fred outrun him?

These thoughts now ran through Fred's mind as he tried to formulate another strategy. Hour after hour, Fred waited motionless in silence, not wanting to give away his position.

It wasn't until Fred began hearing the sound of birds singing did he become aware of the sun rising. It would be a little while longer before the woods would be illuminated enough to travel, but the time was getting close.

Fred did not move until he was able to see a good distance in each direction. Then and only then did he start to get to his feet. The dry leaves cracked loudly in response to each of his steps.

On his feet, Fred started heading toward the main road, stopping only momentarily to catch his breath.

"Clunk!"

The arrow pierced the bark of a nearby tree, embedding itself inches from Fred's heart.

Fred jumped back, startled by the arrow's sudden appearance. Looking in the direction the arrow had

VENGEANCE IS MINE

come from, Fred saw a masked figure dressed completely in black holding a crossbow to his shoulder.

Fred immediately spun around and started running in the opposite direction, pushing himself as hard and as fast as he could.

The assailant had heard Fred when he stopped in the woods. Guessing Fred would not attempt to travel anymore that night, the figure planned to place himself between Fred and the highway. Fred would walk right into him in the morning, and he could force Fred back the opposite way. If Fred chose not to cooperate, he would just kill him early.

He had heard Fred coming. Hiding behind a tree, he waited for the right opportunity. When Fred stopped to rest fifty yards away, it came.

First, he zeroed in on Fred, putting the crosshairs of the scope right between Fred's eyes. Too quick, he thought, then released the arrow and sent the bolt into the tree that Fred leaned against. It worked out just right. Fred darted off in the opposite direction, going farther and farther away from the highway, and help.

Even the most experienced woodsman sometimes became disoriented and unsure of his location, resorting to a compass to determine a correct heading. But without a compass, and compounded by the fact that a madman was trying to kill him, Fred soon became hopelessly lost.

This, he thought, has to be a nightmare, lost in the woods with no form of protection, with a killer hot on your heels.

Fred, exhausted from the run, stopped and sat on a fallen log. His side hurt to the point where he wanted to scream. Touching the area gently, he knew more than one rib had been damaged. But as severe as the pain

VENGEANCE IS MINE

was, Fred knew he had to somehow control it, he had to get away: his life depended on it. As Fred scanned the area, looking among the trees for any sign of his executioner, he detected none. He momentarily fell into a sense of ease, when . . .

Twang!!!

Pain shot through Fred's leg as the arrow pierced his thigh. Falling back off the log, Fred screamed in agony.

Fred picked himself off the ground, just high enough to see over the log. Fred saw the masked figure approach. Fred realized he was about to die.

He stood over Fred with the crossbow drawn and quivering.

Using his foot, he lightly tapped the arrow protruding from Fred's leg.

Fred screamed in pain, trying hard to regain his composure.

"Please, John," Fred said, "I'm sorry about what happened ten years ago," he gasped between his tears of fear and pain. "Killing me won't change anything."

Fred sat up, leaning his shoulder against the log, he looked up at the eyes staring at him through the hood. Fiery, bloodshot eyes pierced Fred like a dagger.

At that point, Fred knew nothing he could say or do would change the inevitable outcome.

Fred saw him release the front of the bow with his left hand, still holding it on Fred with the right. Reaching behind his head, he pulled the hood off.

Fred stared up at his tormentor in shock and disbelief.

Fred said not a word. He only stared in silence, as the executioner once again took aim on Fred, sending an arrow through Fred's body.

VENGEANCE IS MINE

The shock of the moment followed him even into his death. He died with his eyes open, in the shocking disbelief of who the administer of justice was.

The assailant breathed a sigh of relief. The burning anger and hatred which had swollen in the pit of his stomach began to subside.

Judge Parker, Steve, Paul, and Fred were now dead. There was only one left, the one who was ultimately responsible for that night. One left and it would be over. The injustice would be vindicated.

He walked out of the woods, leaving Fred's body to be consumed by the scavengers of the forest. It would not take long before his flesh would be consumed, then his bones scattered throughout the forest.

Walking out, he felt as though a load had been lifted from his chest.

VENGEANCE IS MINE

VENGEANCE IS MINE

Chapter Twenty-five

John, having heard about Burt's death, now stayed even closer to the store and home, 'That's all I need,' John thought, 'some trigger-happy cop blowing me away because of the recent murder spree'

Business had been slow. Folks were scared, scared to go out by themselves. Fear hadn't set in until Burt was murdered. Up until that point, people had calmed their anxiety by justifying in their own minds that those two had finally gotten what was coming to them. But when Burt died, a man who was as well known and as kind as he was, it put the killing in a whole new perspective.

John spent most of the day dusting and straightening up the store. When he reached the knife display he had created a week or so earlier, it reminded him of the fact that his effort and imagination had not netted one sale from the case. But then again, business had been slow.

John looked at the case for ways to make it better. maybe, he thought, the display looked too menacing and less inviting. Maybe instead of having the knife blades sticking out, maybe the handles should be sticking out. maybe if the case was larger, it would attract more attention. Lots of maybes, he knew.

VENGEANCE IS MINE

Display was not an exact science. John finally decided to leave the case as it was. But if there was no action or interest in it, he would change it.

The day dragged by until about four. John's mother gathered up the money and the receipt tickets and headed to the bank as she usually did. Though John and his mother had not been working together very long, there were very distinct duties and responsibilities that each of them was accountable for.

As was the routine, John's mother would make the deposits while John closed up. Since the bank was in the opposite direction from their home, Mrs. Braxton would walk there and back. Then she and John would go home together.

Mrs. Braxton left, and John closed the store behind her.

After returning from the country, the assailant parked a short distance from the store and waited and watched. He would now wait, wait for an opportunity to finalize his business. The death of John Braxton would close the account.

Three hours passed before Mrs. Braxton finally went to the bank. He knew where she was going. He had watched their routine for several days, keeping vigilant watch over them while the police also watched them.

Now would be the best possible time. John was alone and the store was closed.

Like a thief in the night, unseen, and unnoticed, he approached the rear of the hardware store. Removing a small, thin screwdriver from his pocket, he pushed it between the doorframe and the door. Because of the thinness of the blade, it slid in easily. With just a little twist, the door opened.

VENGEANCE IS MINE

Wasting no time, he entered the storeroom quickly, then softly closed the door behind him. Standing in the darkness, he waited, he watched, and he listened.

The little sounds John was making as he straightened up gave the intruder both direction and distance to John.

He walked over to the cloth curtains that were evenly separated down the middle. He peered through them. Seeing John, his eyes got bigger. On the other side of the store, John stood busily straightening up the shelves.

Slowly parting the curtains, he emerged from the storeroom. Removing the pistol from his pocket, he approached his unsuspecting victim. Closer . . . still closer.

John quickly worked to straighten the shelves. Not wanting his mother to wait for him, he hurried about his work. As John worked, a chill ran through him, a sense of someone's presence, though no sound had alerted him. John slowly turned and found himself staring into the barrel of a pistol. The opening of the small caliber pistol seemed the size of a shotgun. Then he focused his eyes away from the gun to the person who held it.

"Mrs. Duet!" John exclaimed. John stood facing her eye to eye. She somehow looked different, hardened in some way. She remained emotionless and just stared at John.

"You're the last one!" Mrs. Duet finally spoke.

John, still very much in shock, did not immediately get the connection until she continued.

"Parker, Steve, Paul, Fred, and now you!" Mrs. Duet stated, her tone menacing, her voice hard.

VENGEANCE IS MINE

"Fred's dead too?" John asked, not believing the deputy could be taken when his guard had apparently been so high.

"Yes, especially Fred! He thought he could hid out in his cabin, but I followed him. I left him for the wild animals."

"But why?" John asked in a pleading tone.

"Why? Because of you, my Lisa's dead, that's why."

"You blame me?"

"If you hadn't brought her to that cane field, it never would have happened."

"That's true, but killing me won't bring your daughter back."

"No, it won't, but knowing that the people responsible for her death have been punished will make it a little easier to live with."

"I understand why you killed Parker, Paul, Steve, and Fred, but why was Burt killed? He never hurt anyone."

"He was sticking his nose where it didn't belong! After I killed Paul, I lost Lisa's barrette. He found it, started putting two and two together. Well, he had to be silenced. You see, John, nothing was going to stop me before I got each one of you. Nothing!"

Mrs. Duet brandished the gun, pointing it at John to make him step back further. John knew at any moment she would pull the trigger. His only hope was to try to postpone the inevitable as long as possible. John tried to keep her talking to buy more time.

"So it was you that sent me the reunion notice in prison," John asked, although already knowing the answer.

"That's right, I wanted you to start remembering."

"But, Mrs. Duet, I loved Lisa too!"

VENGEANCE IS MINE

"'No! If you had loved her, you wouldn't have let those animals do what they did!" A tear formed in her eyes as she started to remember the pain and the loss.

"Why did you wait till now?" John pressed further.

Mrs. Duet look at John and paused a moment, then looked at John once more. "I'll tell you, John. You'll have the benefit of knowing everything, before you die!'

"For one, I wanted to get you all at the same time, and if I had killed them while you were still in prison, I would have become the prime suspect. As it turned out, the police were so busy watching you, it made it easy for me. I'm sure it seemed more than just a coincidence to them that when you returned to town, bodies started piling up."

"What about Judge Parker?" John asked, trying to keep the conversation going.

"Yes, Judge Parker, His Honor. I couldn't wait for him. He sat in judgment over Lisa, rendering his justice, swift and sure. After Lisa died, I went to his house; he let me in. I spent about an hour letting him know what it felt like to be a victim. Then I killed him, tore the place up to make it look like a robbery, then left. I killed him, John, just like I'm going to kill you," Mrs. Duet concluded, tightening her grip on the pistol.

"But with my death, they'll surely trace it back to you," John said, trying to reason with her.

"It doesn't matter anymore! It doesn't matter."

With that, Mrs. Duet's face lost all expression, and she aimed the pistol to John's head.

Just when all seemed lost and death imminent, a loud voice called out.

"No!" Mrs. Braxton yelled.

VENGEANCE IS MINE

Hearing the intruder, Mrs. Duet span around and fired. The bullet tore into the doorframe, missing Mrs. Braxton and splintering the wood.

Seeing it was his mother, John charged at Mrs. Duet before she could get another shot off. Throwing his shoulder into her rib cage, John lifted her off her feet and sent her sailing backward, landing on top of his knife display. As Mrs. Duet fell through the glass, the knives pierced her back. The longer blades tore cleanly through her chest.

Her arm fell to her side, twitching with the last remnants of life that remained. Her eyes fixed and opened on John. He would be the last image she saw.

Mrs. Braxton rushed from the curtains, wrapping her arms around her son. "Are you all right?"

"Yes," John replied, "I'm fine."

Also emerging from behind the curtains were the two surveillance officers.

Seeing the surprise on her son's face, Mrs. Braxton started to explain. "John, I was coming back from the bank when I saw you and Mrs. Duet inside. I immediately ran to the police car for help. I ran to the rear of the store with the two police officer not far behind. I had just gotten to the curtain when I saw her pointing the gun at you. That's when I called out."

"Well, your timing was great," John replied with a sigh of relief. "I'm just glad it's over Mrs. Duet's mind must have snapped when Lisa died. She blamed me for her death. It's amazing how she kept her hatred bottled up inside of her, festering for all these years."

Just then, Detective Clement burst through the curtains.

VENGEANCE IS MINE

"Is everyone all right?" he asked as he entered the room, gun drawn. Seeing Mrs. Duet, he returned his pistol to its holster.

"She's your murderer!" Mrs. Braxton said, speaking first.

"We know," Clement said, reaching into his pocket and pulling out the barrette and photo that Burt had copied.

"That's Lisa's," John exclaimed upon seeing the barrette.

"Yes, it was," Detective Clement agreed. "But before it was Lisa's, it was her mother's."

"We found this at The Courtier a few minutes ago. One of the workers found it in the microfilm room."

Opening up the photo, it showed a picture of Lisa and her mother. Lisa was holding some sort of award.

"It seems Burt was able to put it all together before Mrs. Duet could finish her vendetta, and it cost him his life," Clement reasoned. "It's amazing she was able to keep this hatred bottled up inside of her for all these years."

John and his mother walked away from Mrs. Duet's body, breathing a little easier now. The suspicions were over now, John and his mother would try to start fresh and build a life for themselves and try to bury the ghosts of the past.

VENGEANCE IS MINE

VENGEANCE IS MINE

OTHER GREAT TITLES BY
Ricardo S. Dubois

Ghost Squirrel

Swamp Witch

A Time for Miracles

Crossroads

The Treasure of Jean Lafitte

Vengeance is Mine

Southern Justice

When Destinies Collide

Turnabout

The Mardi Gras Murders

The City Beneath the Sea

Autograph copies available by contacting me at:
craftycajun@yahoo.com

VENGEANCE IS MINE